# Just Like Always

Janie had never had a long stay in the hospital but Courtney had. Both had scoliosis, a curvature of the spine, and both were to be put into a cast. Both would probably need surgery before they went home. But aside from the fact that they were both occupying the same hospital room for the same reason, the two had almost nothing in common. Janie loved to play baseball, and approached everything that came her way with the subtlety of a sledge hammer. Courtney, on the other hand, lived in a fantasy world, Greno. She and her friends even had a Greno club, and she saw beauty and delicacy wherever she looked.

That two so unlike persons should be friends seemed highly unlikely on the day they both arrived at the hospital. In fact their first meeting, in the hospital rest room, with Janie standing on the toilet to read the graffitti on the walls, was anything but promising. Yet drawn together by their common loneliness, their common fears, and their need to share what was happening to them, they slowly came to understand each other. Janie really grasped the meaning of Greno; and Courtney could join Janie in acts of hospital rebellion that never would have occurred to her, and probably would have horrified her, only days before.

In spite of its setting and its serious background, this is a funny book. It is also touching, tender, and warmly human. Finally it is a story about how friendship grows and what love really is.

# JUST
# LIKE
# ALWAYS

———◆———

*Elizabeth-Ann Sachs*

ATHENEUM    1981    NEW YORK

*Library of Congress Cataloging in Publication Data*
Sachs, Elizabeth-Ann.

Just like always.

Summary: Confined to the hospital in casts because of scoliosis, two young girls become best friends in spite of the differences between them.

[1. Scoliosis—Fiction. 2. Hospitals—Fiction. 3. Interpersonal relations—Fiction] I. Title.
PZ7.S1186Ju      [Fic]      81-2289
ISBN 0-689-30859-0      AACR2

*Copyright © 1981 by Elizabeth-Ann Sachs*
*All rights reserved*
*Published simultaneously in Canada by*
  *McClelland & Stewart, Ltd.*
*Composition by American–Stratford Graphic Services,*
  *Brattleboro, Vermont*
*Manufactured by R. R. Donnelley & Sons, Inc.,*
  *Crawfordsville, Indiana*
*Designed by Mary Cregan*
*First Edition*

*To My Mother and Father*

*Just Like Always*

# 1

"Listen, you guys, I have to go to the bathroom. Watch my knapsack, will ya?" Janie Tannenbaum knew it was now or never. She just had to get away from her parents.

Ever since she had started coming to the medical center, Janie had checked out one bathroom in particular on the first floor. It had two little stalls and the best grafitti in the world.

Janie kicked open the outside door and barged through before it swung closed. Only when she was inside did she notice a very pretty girl brushing her long blonde hair at the sink.

Neat hair, thought Janie, shoving her baseball cap back on her own red hair. Without stopping she locked the stall door, settled down on the toilet seat and began reading the stuff at eye level on the wall.

The lock on the other stall door clicked. Janie stood up and studied the back wall. She flushed the water absent-mindedly and stepped up on the seat to see the small print way up high. Resting her arm on the metal divider between the two stalls, she chuckled thinking about what Harold, her best friend at home, would say about the newest additions to the wall. She felt in her jean's jacket pocket but didn't have a pencil. Too bad.

"Wow," she said aloud, "would I ever like to add a line to that remark."

It was then that Janie heard a gasp and looked down. In the other stall the blonde girl stared up, horrified.

"Oooops, sorry about that. I wasn't spying, just reading the walls!" The girl did not believe it, Janie could tell. She jumped off the toilet, flushed a couple more times, then crouched down.

The girl's black pumps were still there. "Okay," she yelled under the divider, "I'll go first." She unlocked the stall and bolted out the bathroom door.

"I was just coming in to get you," her mother said. "It was taking such a long time I thought there might be a problem. Places where anyone can walk in sometimes attract strange people. I was a little concerned."

Janie rolled her eyes. "Helene, you worry too much."

"Well come on then. They've got a wheelchair waiting to take you up to your room."

"I don't need it."

"It's a hospital regulation or something. Besides they're fun to race around in once you get the knack." Mrs. Tannenbaum put her arm around Janie's shoulders, and they matched giant steps all the way down the corridor.

"I think," said the nurse at the admitting desk, "that you are going up to Babies on the third floor. Just sit in that wheelchair and I'll check." She gestured with the files in hand.

"BABIES!" Janie's voice rose. "Why'd you stick me with a bunch of babies? I'm in fifth grade. And what do I need a wheelchair for? There's nothing wrong with my legs." She glared at the nurse.

"Go on, Janie." Her father nodded at the chair. "You'll love it."

"But why? There's nothing wrong with my—"

"Janie." Mrs. Tannenbaum spoke firmly.

The nurse came around the side of the desk. "Be a good girl, and I'll let you push yourself."

"Babies!" Janie muttered and threw herself into the rubbery brown seat of the wheelchair. She played with the large wheels, discovering how to roll the chair around the floor, then headed toward the elevator. "Okay. Let's get the show on the road."

From the elevator door on the third floor, Janie went soaring down the hall. When she saw room 318K, she braked hard. The wheelchair jerked to a halt just inside the empty hospital room. "Not bad." Janie checked the brown linoleum floor for skid marks.

"I'm glad I wasn't riding shotgun on that thing," Mrs. Tannenbaum said coming through the door. She dropped Janie's gear on one of the beds.

Janie toured the room on wheels. "Hey, what's this?" She dragged a yellow plastic pan out of the cabinet next to the bed.

"It's a bedpan," said the nurse who had brought the Tannenbaum's up to Janie's room. "If you can't go down the hall to use the bathroom, then you use a bedpan. After you've finished, a nurse will take it away."

"Gross," said Janie. "Really gross." She slammed the cabinet door and pulled open the top drawer. "And what's all this stuff?"

"My, my," said the nurse, "don't we have lots of questions!"

"Janie, where do you want these?" Mr. Tannenbaum carried in a large box full of baseball tropies.

"On the nightstand," said Janie revolving backwards in her wheelchair.

The nurse leaned against the bed and took the items out one at a time. "This is a thermometer. Your temperature will be checked two or three times each day. And this is—"

"Why?" Janie stopped short. "I don't have a cold. I have a bend in my spine. Ever hear of scoliosis? You don't get a fever from it. It's not even catching. Don't you guys know anything?"

The woman nodded her head and tried smiling. "Yes, Janie . . . but while you're in the hospital, your temperature will be checked, regularly."

"Okay, okay." Janie shrugged. "What else is there?"

"A washpan to clean yourself when you're bedridden. Also a plastic pitcher and cup for water." She held the items up and then put everything away. "And if you have any more questions, this little buzzer lights up in the nurses' office when you press it. Someone will always answer. Make sure you don't overdo it, though. Now, I really must get going. If you'll just get out of the wheelchair and change into your pajamas—"

"How come I have to wear PJ's? I'm not going to bed now. It's only five o'clock."

"No, but patients don't wear street clothing in the hospital." Suddenly, the nurse laughed. "Janie, Janie, wait till the people on this floor get to know you." Shaking her white-capped head, she smiled down at Janie. "I have a funny feeling you'll keep this place hopping."

With that she pried Janie out of the wheelchair, turned it around and started for the door. "Stay out of mischief if you can, Janie Tannenbaum." She winked and was gone.

"Well," said Janie, turning to her parents, "she was something else!"

"Janie," her father said, "ask all the questions you like. But don't bother them with things you can figure out for yourself."

Mrs. Tannenbaum nodded. "They have lots to do around here. Don't make a pest of yourself, Cookie. We're going to have to leave now. I noticed a phone booth at the end of the hall, near the waiting room. Call at night when we're home. You know we won't be able to visit every day because of work and the distance. But we'll be here on the weekends."

Ignoring the uneasy feeling in her stomach, Janie said, "I'll walk you guys down to the elevator. Okay?"

Grabbing both her parents around the waist, Janie tried skipping between them as they walked. They laughed as they all stumbled down the hall.

"You'll be fine. You know that, Janie." Mr. Tannenbaum bent and kissed her on the forehead. Then he rumpled her frizzy hair.

Janie nodded, trying hard to feel that way. She pushed the down button and studied the flashing numbers as the elevator climbed. "When will you be back?"

"Soon, Janie. Very soon. I promise you," Mrs. Tannenbaum said, hugging her. "If you're homesick, sing our favorite tune, the one we almost made up. You won't feel so far from us."

The light over the elevator flashed a red three.

The doors rolled back. "We have to go now, Honey. Don't forget to call."

Janie listened to the humming sound that carried her parents away. "Bye, you guys," she whispered.

For a moment Janie watched the canvas bumps rise and fall as she curled up her toes and pressed them out flat inside her sneakers. Then clasping her hands on top of her head, she began singing. "Ta . . . daa . . . dada . . . ta . . . daa . . . dada. . . ."

Skipping around the corner, Janie stopped short. With squinting eyes and thrust up chin, she studied the long green corridor. Its length was broken by doorways, and at the far end a rectangular room crossed the hall, creating a gigantic T.

"Okay, hospital." Janie addressed the hall. "I'm giving you an examination for a change. It won't hurt. I'll just work my way down one side and up the other. Now, take a deep breath."

When the first door swung open, only a plump nurse with curly auburn hair glanced up. A group of interns in white smocks were taking notes as the chief resident lectured. Janie moved on quickly, ducking into the bathroom next.

She stepped into one of the gigantic bathtubs and stretched out. "Hiya, kid. Want to get in this boat with me?"

A toddler in blue flannel pajamas stuck a thumb in her small mouth. Her brown eyes stared at Janie's.

"Come on, jump in. I'll take you for a ride."

The little girl fled. On a long red and white string she dragged an upturned black train.

"Hey, I'm not that bad!" Janie laughed and climbed out. Then catching her reflection in a mirror over the sink, she stuck out her tongue. She did her best ugly faces with her favorite grunting sounds.

"Are you ill?" A face appeared next to Janie's in the mirror.

"Naa," said Janie, talking to the nurse's anxious-looking reflection. "I'm just checking this place out. I got here a little while ago."

"You're sure?" The nurse giggled. "I really didn't know what I should do. I'm new here, too. I started working on this floor yesterday. I'm Miss Parker." She pointed proudly to her name badge. "What's your name?"

"Janie," said Janie, trying to read "Parker" backwards in the mirror.

"Well, if you need anything, please let me know."

"Right-O, Miss Parker."

"By the way"—Miss Parker stopped in the doorway—"have you seen the playroom, Janie? You should. There are lots of wonderful dolls and games."

Janie dashed out after her. "I haven't played dolls since kindergarten," she yelled after the nurse.

"Miss Tannenbaum! This is not the ball park.

There are many sick children on this floor. Would you mind lowering your voice?"

Janie swung around. A huge woman in a stiff white uniform frowned at her.

"And when do you plan to change your clothes? That was the first thing you were told. We have rules, and they must be kept."

"I only wanted to see where things were." Janie looked the nurse in the eye.

"Do as you are told, miss. Go straight to your room and put on a hospital gown or your own things. And stay there. It's dinnertime. Now march!"

Boy, Janie thought, she acts like she owns this whole place. Not daring to look over her shoulder, she hurried down the hall, planning to finish the tour later, when the coast was clear.

In the doorway of 318K, however, she hesitated. There was a girl sitting on the other hospital bed. Janie could tell she had already put her things away and changed her clothes. Janie also knew exactly who she was.


Courtney sat on the edge of the bed, facing the window, but her eyes were closed. Long blonde hair that had never been cut fell around her shoulders, almost touching the bed. Fragile hands rested gracefully in her lap, among the orange folds of a long silky nightgown.

If only, she thought, her friends could see

her now. They would be sorry they hadn't made her Great-Grand Wizard of their secret club. Courtney knew she deserved to be head. She had been the first one with the idea of a Fantasy Club. She'd even read all the books about the creation and destruction of Greno. Besides, Courtney decided, she looked more like the queen of Greno than Shelly did.

Courtney pushed all that out of her mind and began beckoning, the club's most important ritual. She rubbed a small silver disk, known to possess great magical powers.

Silently she addressed her friend. Marguerite of the Sea, open your mind. Do not block me out. I wish to speak. Marguerite, I am trying to reach you. Are you listening? I am here in the high tower of the white wizards. They have done me no harm. My parents have been sent away. I tried not to cry when they waved to me from the street, but I wanted to. You would too, you know. It's scary being left, even after it's happened so many times. Marguerite, are you listening to me? You promised you would try. Please beckon to me. You are my friend, and we have to keep working on this. If Shelly and Melanie can do it, we just have to. Pretty soon we will be able to actually speak inside one another's minds, like in Greno. But we have to practice. Don't make best friends with anyone else while I'm here, okay? I'll try again later.

Courtney swayed back and forth on her bed

to the enchanted music only creatures of Greno could hear. Softly she sang, mouth open, eyes closed. She continued fingering the silver disk with the bird on it.

"Goodbye, Marguerite. I hope you have heard me," Courtney said aloud, the last part of the beckoning ritual. She opened her eyes and was stunned to see that disgusting girl who had been in the bathroom downstairs. She was leaning on the rail at the foot of the bed.

"Who's Marguerite?" Janie demanded.

"My friend at home. And whom, may I ask, are you?"

"My name," said Janie, touching the brim of her baseball cap, "is Janie Tannenbaum. My name means Christmas tree in a song, but I'm Jewish. Who are you?"

"I am Courtney-Ann Schaeffer, Arch-Queen of the Fantasy Club. You may call me Courtney-Ann. I have a secret name that I can't tell you because that would give you complete power over me."

"Oh," said Janie, scratching her head, "do you have a nickname?"

"Yes, but that's my secret name, and I cannot tell you without endangering myself."

"Wouldn't be something dumb like Rumple-stiltskin?"

"No," said Courtney, shaking her head.

"How many guesses do I get?"

"As many as you need."

"Why don't you just tell me?"

"Because . . . that would give you complete—"

"You really believe stuff like that?"

"I belong to a secret club at home, and we do magical things. I write it all down so I'll always remember. Writing is the best part."

"What kind of things does this fantasy club do?"

For a moment Courtney said nothing. Janie imagined her running around in the woods in a long white slip and phoney homemade wings.

"I can't tell you, but have you ever read the stories about the kingdom of Greno?"

"No, mostly I read books about baseball and some mysteries. And I'm on the team at school. Ever play baseball?"

"No, I'm not allowed to take gym. I could lend you one of my books, if you want to read about Greno. But you'll have to be very careful because my things are magical. Don't ever touch anything without asking me. You could get hurt."

"Okay," said Janie, taking in the black wooden box, the large pink seashell and the magenta candles on the nightstand. "But would you tell me one thing? What did you mean before when you said about Marguerite hearing you? Were you doing ESP?"

"Ahh . . . well, sort of . . . I . . . ."

"I know, I know," said Janie rolling her eyes,

"you can't tell me because it's dangerous. Right?"

"I'm not really sure if I should."

Janie shrugged. "Are you going to be in this room?"

"Yes, this is the room I'm always in. I've been here so many times that I think of it as mine. I was hoping I'd be alone."

"Sorry about that." Janie resisted commenting on the fat brown and green leather frog on Courtney's pillow. "This isn't exactly my first time either, you know. I was here before for x-rays and tests. I'm having a cast put on because of my scoliosis, and then I'm having an operation." Janie paused. "So, what's wrong with you?"

Courtney looked down at the silver medallion in her hand. "I . . . thought I was the only one in the world who needed to be . . . in a cast. I never knew anyone else who had a curvature of the spine."

Janie was surprised to hear that. She knew a whole bunch of kids at school who wore corrective braces, though she was the only one who needed a body cast. But so what! Janie figured she'd be missing a whole lot of school and that sounded terrific. "Maybe that's why they stuck us together. Have you ever seen what the cast looks like?"

"Only in a picture. It's horrible."

Janie laughed. "My father says it looks like a turtle shell for a person. It's sort of funny."

"Miss Tannenbaum!" Janie knew the voice. "You still have not changed your clothing? What must I do to make you obey the rules?"

The nurse stood in the doorway, arms folded across her broad chest. "I want to check both your charts, and the dinner trays are out in the hall." She invaded their room with an armload of clipboards and papers.

"Good evening, Mrs. Bickerstaff," Courtney said politely.

"I'm glad to see you have done as you were told." Mrs. Bickerstaff gave Courtney her automatic smile. "You have always been a model patient when you've visited us."

Janie scurried over to her side of the room. She dumped the stuff in her sack on the bed. Her baseball with the autographs rolled over the edge and thudded onto the floor. "Babies," Janie muttered as she scrambled under the bed.

# 2

---

"Want to go snooping around?" Janie asked later that evening. "I heard Mrs. Bickerstaff saying good night, so I think it's safe."

"No, thank you." Courtney turned from the window. Her long orange robe, with its oriental collar and the frog clasps, whirled around her legs. "I'll stay here and write." She took a small pewter elf from a carefully arranged circle of stones on the nightstand and sat on her bed.

"Okay. See you later." Janie, in red flannel pajamas, sneakers and her old baseball cap, marched out.

The corridor was deserted and the entire floor quiet, with a just-before-bedtime feel. Janie considered the idea that she was not supposed to be prowling around.

But, making a dash for the far end of the hall, she slipped into the Babies' Ward. Dark and warm, it smelled of talcum powder and wet diapers. Janie heard an infant whimper as she crept through the ward and into the deserted playroom.

The black shapes of toys crouched in the darkness. When Janie stepped on a squeaky toy train, she decided to end her investigation. "Rats," she mumbled. "It's too early to go to bed."

She tiptoed past the nurses' station, through the waiting room and into a phone booth. It was dark and stuffy inside. As she closed the door behind her, the overhead light went on and the fan started whirring. She opened the door quickly and waited to see if anyone came out of the office.

"Swell," Janie muttered. "If you shut the door, the fan and light go on. And if you open the door, you can't see. What a place!"

She closed the door again, threw money in the coin box and dialed the number. Then opening the door, she waited in the dark for someone to answer.

"Hello?"

"Hi! It's Janie. How's it going?"

"Janie who?"

"What do you mean Janie who? You dummy, Harold, I only left this afternoon." Janie heard her friend snicker. "I have to whisper or I'll get caught."

"What do you mean? Is it like prison?"

"No, not exactly. But it's lights-out, like camp, and I'm supposed to be in bed now. There's no way I'm going to bed."

"Yeah, that's nuts."

"Tell me what happened with the spitball contest?"

"It was fantastic! Our team won, but Mrs. Moran found out."

"Oh . . . jeez, Har."

"Yeah, you got it. She made us all write, 'Spitting is a rude and unsocial act.' One hundred and fifty times. After school too. I missed practice."

"Nice goin', Harold. Just like a second-grader."

"You're lucky you got to go in the hospital today. I'm not kidding. Nobody would sit next to me on the bus."

"Nobody made them do it. We were just goofing. Those jerks. I wish you were here."

"What's it like? Did they do anything to you yet?"

"No. It's okay so far. Tomorrow I have more x-rays. Harold!" Janie suddenly remembered. "You wouldn't believe the weirdo in my room. A space cadette! She brought all this junk—like frogs and shells, all kinds of creepy twigs. Even two real bird wings. And, the best part is, she says she can do magic or ESP. She's here for the same exact thing as me, but I think it's her head that needs work. All she talks about is her Fantasy Club and a place called Greno! Ever hear of it?"

"Nope."

"I really wish you were here instead of her. We could have a terrific time. They have these super wheelchairs. You can make them go around in circles. Makes you sicker than the kindergarten merry-go-round."

"Sounds neat. Maybe I could sneak in sometime. I'll get a lab coat from school and a pair of my father's glasses. I could pretend I'm a doctor."

"Harold, do it! Listen . . . I better go before I'm caught. I'll call you again."

"Okay."

"Say 'Hi' to the kids. Bye, Har."

"See ya."

"Hey, wait a minute."

"Yeah?"

"Are you going to pull any of our numbers with anyone else while I'm here?"

"Are you kidding? Who? Come on! Quit being a baby."

"Yeah, you're right. Okay, see ya!"

"Bye."

Janie hung up the phone and waited for a few minutes. She wanted to be sure the coast was clear. It was quiet when she slipped out of the booth. The only sound was the soft jangling noise made by the coins in her pocket.

The candy machine inside the waiting room caught Janie's eye. Fingering her change, she paused to study all the different wrappers. She was hungry. Only a pig would have eaten that supper. Finally she dropped in a coin and pulled one of the handles. There was the rattle of money falling into the machine, the handle crashing into place, the thud of candy dropping down.

As the sounds bounced off the walls, Janie stood paralyzed, waiting for a nurse to come charging out of the office. Nothing happened. She waited some more. "How dumb can you be?" Janie asked herself. After what seemed like a long time, she grabbed the candy bar.

But just then a squeaking noise came from the hall. She froze again. And in the eerie glow of the exit light, she saw a door open.

"Janie," a voice said, "is that you?"

Turning, Janie saw Courtney peeking out of the waiting room lavatories. "Courtney," said Janie, relieved, "what are you doing in the men's room?"

"I was writing and got hungry so I came down for something to eat. When I heard the door of the phone booth open, I got scared so I hid. Is it really the men's room? I'm starved out of my mind. My mother forgot to bring food."

"I am too," said Janie, "and that thing makes so much noise. . . ."

"I heard it."

"I wouldn't try it again. Someone might hear. I'll give you some of mine if . . ."

"Oh, thank you."

". . . if you go for a walk with me." Janie

tore off the wrapper and shoved it into her pocket. "Come on."

"We can't . . . we could get in trouble if the nurse goes in our room. Everybody's supposed to be in bed, now."

Janie leaned against the exit door and munched on the top half of the candy bar. "What could they do to us?" she asked with a mouthful of chocolate and nuts.

"I don't know, but I don't want to get in trouble," Courtney said, watching the candy disappear.

"Maybe they'll punish us and make us go home?"

A startled look crossed Courtney's face, then she giggled. "Okay. Give me half."

Janie handed Courtney the candy and went on thinking. The caramel stuck to the side of her teeth. She pushed the sticky stuff around with her tongue. Salted nuts with caramel and chocolate was her favorite candy, after peanut butter and chocolate. She popped the last bite into her mouth.

"You know what we could do," she said, trying to size up Courtney. "We could get another candy bar and hide out on the landing." Janie nodded her head toward the door. "No one would look out there if they heard the noise."

Courtney was just hungry enough to give in. "All right," she said, slowly licking away the last of the chocolate on her thumb.

"I'll tell you what. You hold the door open, and I'll do the machine. That'll be even faster."

Courtney opened the heavy metal door as Janie decided on their second choice. Just as Janie was about to throw the money in, Courtney whispered, "Wait! Suppose this door locks behind us. We won't be able to get back in. Let's try it first."

Janie rolled her eyes. "Okay, go outside and I'll open it for you."

"No, let me open it from out there. Then we'll know."

"Okay, okay." Janie sighed.

"You'll open it for me, won't you, if it locks?"

"I'll open it," Janie said in exasperation. "Just get out there."

Courtney let the door close. As soon as it clicked into place, she opened it. It was not locked. "Okay. We're all set."

Janie let the coin go. Her other hand was ready to pull.

Janie and Courtney settled just below the dimly lit second-floor landing. "Just in case," Courtney had said. From the stairs they could see a bridge framed in the window. With its flood lights on, the bridge stood out against the darkness.

"So tell me about Greno," Janie said, leaning back and resting her elbows on the top stair.

After a long hesitation, Courtney said, "Greno is a magical place that exists right beside us. You only have to learn to see it."

"I don't understand." Janie made a face. "If I'm there, how come I don't know about it?"

Courtney sat thinking about Greno. It was so special that talking about it felt scary, as if she was giving it away. And yet she wanted Janie to like her and not think Greno was a stupid baby game. "Do you really want to see Greno?" she asked finally.

"Yeah, sure," Janie said, not knowing what to expect. "Show me."

"See that bridge? When I was very little, my grandmother had an apartment in the city. You could see that same bridge from her bedroom window. Once she told me it was a strand of diamonds with two rubies for a clasp. I even remember her saying it was mine, but I had to leave it there. If you look at it, just right, it's a necklace in a black velvet box! That's how you find Greno."

"Oh, wow!" Janie roared, staring out the window. "I can see it, a gigantic necklace hanging out there in the night! I never think of things like that. It was only a bridge on the way to the hospital for me."

Courtney stopped looking out the window. "I was scared to tell you. I thought you would laugh. I never told anyone about that bridge being a necklace, not even my friends in the club. It's always been my secret, to look for whenever I'm here."

"Tell me more stuff like that. I want to do it again." Janie wiggled around on the concrete.

"If you squint your eyes—"

"So, this is where the pajama party is!" A voice at the top of the stairs interrupted the conversation.

Janie and Courtney looked up. A nurse was standing on a stair above them. Neither girl moved.

"You must be the missing Courtney and Janie. I've been looking all over for the two of you," she said, coming down the stairs and leaning on the banister. "I'd just about given up. I figured you had skipped town, so I decided to walk down to the security guards' station when I couldn't reach them on the phone."

For once Janie was speechless. She couldn't believe how beautiful this woman was with her jet black hair and dark skin. But most of all it was her eyes that held Janie. She had never seen eyes that were black green.

Courtney was surprised also. The nurse wasn't scolding, but instead was sitting down on the landing between them.

Tucking a dark strand of hair under her uniform cap, she said, "Isn't that view magnificent?"

Janie exploded with conversation. "We were just talking about that bridge," she said, studying the woman's profile. "Courtney has this terrific game! Tell her about the bridge," Janie urged.

"Her," said the nurse, "has a name. I'm Ms. Rogers. And you must be Janie?"

"Ahhh . . . sorry. Yeah, I'm Janie and she's Courtney. Courtney tell Ms. Rogers!"

Courtney's arms tightened around her drawn up legs, hugging them closer to her chest. She stared out the window.

Ms. Rogers filled the awkward silence. "I usually work the late shift and I like watching the bridge and the sky. I love how they look in the changing light, especially near morning."

"Courtney," said Janie insistently, "if you don't tell, then I will."

"If Courtney doesn't want to, that's all right."

"But she just told me!"

Courtney looked away from the window. "It was just a dumb idea that the bridge looked like a necklace." Abruptly, she stood up. "I want to go back to the room. I have important things to do."

No one spoke in the darkened corridor. Janie glanced at Courtney. What was the matter with her, anyway. She was really strange.

There was only silence until Janie and Courtney were tucked into bed.

"Well, good night, you two. Pleasant dreams," Ms. Rogers said, and she disappeared into the dark hall.

Janie flopped over on her stomach and snuggled up to the scratchy pillow. "Good night, Courtney-Ann Schaeffer, Arch-Queen of the Greno Fantasy club."

Courtney sat at the foot of her bed, concentrating on the starless sky. Fingering a black and gold book, she started to beckon. Marguerite of the Sea, open your mind to me. I'll never have another friend like you.

# 3

———◆———

"Dr. Pix. Dr. Pix. Call for Dr. Pix on line 2214. Dr. Pix, please pick up on 2214." The voice on the intercom drifted softly through the shadowy morning hall.

"Dr. Fix, Dr. Wix, Dr. Mix." Janie mimicked, falling backwards across the foot of the bed. Her arms and head dangling over the edge, she studied the floor from her upside-down position. Mostly there were legs: bed legs, table legs, chair legs. A woman with hairy legs and oxford shoes was making up Courtney's bed.

Janie wondered where the nurse had wheeled off Her Majesty. That event and the sun blazing through the windows had shattered Janie's early morning sleep. And then, just as she had been drifting off again, the food carts began rattling out in the hall. Finally, smelling the food, Janie had decided she might as well sit up and take a look at it.

But it was absolutely the worst mess she had ever seen. Courtney had said the food was always bad, and she had been right about that. Meals might be the only thing they agreed upon.

Something hit the floor with a thud. Janie saw a lady with a pink uniform picking up a black leather notebook. It was trimmed in gold with the word "Diary" stamped across the front.

"Now, where'd you come from?" The woman spoke to the book. "Out of the pillowcase? That's mighty strange." She placed it on top of the nightstand, gave the sheet a final tug, and carried off a pile of laundry.

Janie sat up, then hopped out of bed barefooted. Halfway across the room she changed her mind and turned to the window. Resting her head on her arms along the deep windowsill, she thought about Courtney.

Secret names? Greno? Dangerous magical things? How could anybody believe in that? And yet for a second last night, the bridge had been a necklace. But there was no such place as Greno. And that was only a pile of junk on the nightstand. "I could touch any of it if I wanted to. Nothing would happen to me. It's all a bunch of mumbo-jumbo."

Janie taunted the frog on Courtney's pillow, "Hey, beanbag, if I kiss you, will you turn into a handsome prince?"

She climbed up on a chair and then onto the wide sill. Below on the street there were dirty pigeons scuttling around where mounds of gray snow had been plowed back. The sidewalks were icy and rutted. It looked cold with the trees whipping about and the sky so bleak. Janie could see the city moving out in every direction, and it all looked cold. Again the nagging memory of Courtney welled up. Janie shoved the huge window open. She just couldn't figure her out!

Startled by someone's loud gasp, Janie clung to the window sash to steady herself. "Miss Tannenbaum, what are you doing?"

Janie did not have to look to know who was standing behind her, once again. Deliberately crossing her arms over her chest like the nurse, Janie leaned on the glass. "I'm opening the window," she said, staring down at Mrs. Bickerstaff.

The woman had trouble containing herself. "Get down," she demanded. "And if you want a window opened, ask!"

Janie spoke as nonchalantly as possible. "Mrs. Bickerstaff," she said, standing on the chair now at eye level with the nurse, "what exactly is your function around here?" She used her father's business voice.

One of the nurse's steel gray eyebrows arched. "I am the charge nurse, Missy. So watch your step. I don't like troublemakers! Now sit down. I have to do temperatures this morning, and I want to check yours."

Janie knew enough not to question that again. "Do I have a temperature?" she asked through clenched teeth, holding the thermometer under her tongue.

"You had better hope so! If you don't, you're dead!"

"You're kidding!" The glass hit the floor with a tinkling splatter. "I always thought—"

"Now look what you've done. Don't you know that you're supposed to keep your mouth shut?"

"Yeah, but you said—"

"And mercury is impossible to pick up once it scatters. Nurses out sick, paper work to do; I can tell this is going to be one of those days." She stooped down, talking to herself, and began picking up the glass.

Janie got the brown metal wastebasket from under the sink and brought it back. "Why is it so hard to pick up?" she asked, kneeling on the floor.

"Put on your slippers and stay away." Mrs. Bickerstaff spoke without lifting her capped head.

Janie shoved her feet into her sneakers and squatted down at a little distance, studying the nurse's attempts to push the mercury onto a piece of paper. Each time she touched the quivering gray balls, they fractured into smaller and smaller fragments.

"That's really neat stuff."

"Go eat," Mrs. Bickerstaff said, not looking at Janie. "And don't get any ideas. Mercury is poisonous."

Janie had thought the same thing about breakfast. As before, she studied the rubbery scrambled eggs, then began rearranging them with a fork. She decided the little-pieces-scattered-over-the-plate design was the best. It almost looked as if she'd eaten.

Then, because Mrs. Bickerstaff was watching, Janie gulped down the warm orange juice. It was the only thing she could stand. What would happen if the nurse decided to stay till she'd finished every bit of breakfast? Janie stabbed the cold, rigid bacon. It splintered.

"You know, Janie, it would behoove you to be a little more like Courtney Schaeffer. She is very sweet and quiet. She'd never climb on windows and break thermometers. And she's not acting fresh because she has to be in the hospital. Look at her things all neatly arranged."

Janie studied her own stuff piled on the nightstand and thrown over her chair. Miss Prissy Perfect, Janie thought, banging her heels against the bed rails. Everybody's little darling!

"Try to be more like her, why don't you? She's such a lovely child."

No way, Janie thought later, marching into Courtney's side of the room. Boldly, she placed her hands on the oriental tea caddy. "So explode," she dared the black box. "Go ahead and do it."

When nothing happened, Janie lifted the black and gold diary off the stand, wondering about the kind of junk Courtney wrote. She plopped on Courtney's bed with her back to the empty room and opened the diary to the last page that had been written on. The small, delicate handwriting filled the pale blue lines. She read quickly.

BABIES

MARCH

*Dear Courtney,*

*Here I am in the hospital again. It's like all the other times. Same horrid smells. Food's as bad as ever. And good 'ole Mrs. Bickerstaff is still around. She's the only person I know from the last time. It's the same in ways I don't want and different in ways I don't want. If only it were a bad dream. Then I could wake up and it would be all over. . . .*

*This time there's a girl in the room with me called Janie. Marguerite would never hang around with her because of the crazy way Janie acts. But Marguerite has never been in a hospital, and she doesn't know anything about what happens to you here. Marguerite would be scared, and Janie isn't. She's brave. She's not even afraid of Mrs.*

*Bicker! And I like the crazy way she acts!*

*I'm not sure that Janie likes me, but I really want her to. I just don't know what to do about it. . . .*

*Well, I have to go now. I'm starving. The only good thing about this place is that there's still a candy machine.*

*Bye for now,*
*CAS*

Janie stopped reading and closed the book without looking down at it again. Putting one untied sneaker on the floor, then the other, she stood up, feeling, suddenly, that someone was watching her. She replaced the diary where it had been and then very slowly turned around. No one was there.

She retreated to her side of the room and belly flopped onto the bed. What was that all about, that stuff in Courtney's diary? She had thought that Courtney was like those stuck-up girls at school who were always combing their hair in the bathrooms and showing off . . . having secrets and clubs . . . acting better than everyone else just because they were pretty. Why hadn't Courtney said anything about how she felt? Did she really believe that ESP junk worked?

"Excuse me, are you Tannenbaum?" A man with greasy blond hair and dark glasses stood in the doorway.

"Who wants to know?" Janie rolled over and sat up.

"Look, I'm supposed to take a J. Tannenbaum down for x-rays this morning. And I can't read the room number scribbled on this sheet. Are you the patient or not?"

Janie looked him up and down. "Next room," she said hopping off the bed and going to the window.

Nothing at all made sense to Janie. She wouldn't even have known that Courtney . . . Cass—whoever she was . . . wanted to be friends, if she hadn't looked. A jumble of thoughts flew around in Janie's head, and her stomach felt queasy.

"Nice try, kid." Janie turned around to see the man pushing a wheelchair into the room. And Mrs. Bickerstaff was standing right beside him.


Nothing was working for Courtney this morning as she lay on a stretcher table in an unfamiliar green hall. She had memorized every crack in the unfriendly ceiling, awaiting and dreading the sound of her name being called. It seemed like hours ago that she had been left alone in this chilly corridor outside some swinging wooden doors.

She had tried beckoning to Marguerite, but Janie's freckled face kept appearing. She couldn't get rid of it, and she did not want to think about Janie.

Closing her eyes, Courtney tried again. She was the kidnapped princess trapped in a dark sea cave. The people of Greno would search for her but might not arrive in time. The tide was rising in the cave. The gathering seaweed would smother her.

Courtney's fantasy was broken abruptly as the table began rolling on its rubber wheels. Viewing the dimly lit auditorium beyond the opened doors, she knew the Grens had not heard her.

The room was crowded with men and women dressed in white smocks who sat in curved tiered rows, which disappeared into the darkness. The stretcher table was stationed under bright spotlights at the front end of the room.

Courtney could not see beyond the glare but felt eyes upon her. The rough hospital gown clung to her damp shoulders, and she began beckoning frantically.

Marguerite, you are of the sea. Save me! This cave is filled with white-eyed monsters who will devour me! Speak to me now!

"Courtney . . ." a voice dragged her away from beckoning. She opened her eyes, wanting the nightmare to be over.

Everything was still there, but Courtney recognized a face. "Dr. Michaels?" She hadn't known he'd be there. As she smiled at the man with ash brown hair and purple-gray eyes,

Courtney didn't realize she was blushing. She was to be saved by the King of Greno, himself. Courtney knew he had left behind his magical emerald cloak with the black and white ermine tails. Disguised as one of the monsters, Courtney realized that they would not recognize him for what he was.

". . . these people are studying to be doctors, and they're interested in your medical problems. I want to show them your back and talk about your medical history. It will only take a few moments."

Courtney nodded, the fantasy evaporating. She said nothing, but really she didn't want to do what he asked. She hated to have anybody see her ugly red scars and tilted shoulders. Yet she pulled the frayed tiestrings at the back of the white wrinkled gown. Would Janie have said no to him if she didn't want to?

The doctor began his lecture. "Courtney has a rather pronounced curvature of the spine that developed after a tumor was discovered and removed during infancy. Until now there has been little physical discomfort and no severe disabilities. However, the usual treatment of scoliosis by corrective braces has not halted the progression of the spinal curve. A full body cast is now necessary and surgery is also likely for. . . "

Dr. Michaels talked on and on, gently fingering her exposed back. Courtney's attention slipped away after a few moments. She didn't like listening to it; and she knew it all by heart, anyway. The thought of Janie returned. This time Courtney remembered her own pleasure when Janie saw the bridge as a necklace last night. It had been such a surprise . . . why did she have to open her big mouth and tell. . . .

People were beginning to leave the hall when Courtney became aware of a voice consulting with Dr. Michaels. It was Dr. Pix, who had performed her first operation. Engrossed in conversation, he simply patted her shoulder.

He did that instead of smiling, she knew. Even though he had a stern voice and always seemed angry, Courtney liked him. After reading all the tales about Greno, she understood that he was the same as the mean Riddler of the Tower who in the end wasn't mean at all.

"Do you mind if I ride up to the third floor with you, Courtney?" Dr. Michaels asked, interrupting her thoughts. "You can tell me how you're doing on the way."

Blushing again, Courtney stretched out on her side with one bent arm supporting her head. As the double doors opened into the hall, people stood aside for the table to pass. Courtney recalled a picture of a famous queen borne on a chaise at the head of a procession.

"Oh . . . goodbye, Dr. Pix," she called, fluttering her hand. The small man with the white hair and full white beard solemnly nodded his head.

# 4

Janie swooped into the chair beside Courtney's bed. "Well, hello!" she gushed. "How's it going?"

Courtney turned away from the nightstand with the diary in her hand. Frowning, she considered Janie: the hair sticking out of her baseball cap, the pale skin mottled with pale freckles, the wide, flat nose and hazel eyes, the plaid robe and untied sneakers. Courtney fingered her diary.

Janie met Courtney's unflinching stare. She must know, Janie thought, trying to ignore her stomachache. But suddenly, Janie remembered the lady with hairy legs. Courtney couldn't know. There was no way. "If you're wondering about that book of yours, some lady was changing the sheets this morning. She dropped it on the floor. I saw her put it on the nightstand."

"Did she open it?" There was an edge in Courtney's voice.

"No." Janie's stomach rumbled loudly.

Courtney dropped on her bed, she did not let go of the diary.

"Sooo . . ." Janie said at the end of a long sigh. "Where were you this morning?"

Courtney rolled over on her back and stared at the ceiling. "They took me . . . to a dark and dangerous underground cave. I only escaped because the magic I've learned is awfully powerful. I can't talk about it now. I'm very tired."

Janie hesitated. "At least you got to miss breakfast. Mrs. Bickerstaff made me eat it. I could have used some magic to get rid of her this morning."

Janie wrapped her arms over her head and looked out the door. "They brought you back in time for lunch, though. I can smell it crawling down the hall. Could you work up a little charm so that that stuff can't get through the door? Like an invisible shield or something? I'll absolutely die if I have to eat another gross meal." Holding her throat with both hands, Janie slid down in the chair. She made gagging sounds as she thrashed around, stomping the linoleum. "A spell, a spell," she choked.

Courtney was about to ask Janie to quit making fun of her. But when she saw Janie down on the floor, squirming and gasping, she could not keep from laughing.

"I'll die! I'll die!" Janie rasped.

Thumbing through her journal, Courtney assumed her magical position. "Here within, an ancient spell to change the dreaded lunch into the wonderous food eaten in the fallen land of Greno!"

Janie's writhing halted. She sat up. "They had food?"

"Yes," said Courtney knowingly, "there was noy, a green creamy dip, and black jeuuy seeds that they mixed into it."

"Blahh." Janie's tongue hung out. "Doesn't sound much better."

"It was probably worse." Courtney laughed at Janie sitting on the floor.

"I think," said Janie after the food trays arrived, "we should go out for lunch." The sight plus the smell was not helping her upset stomach. She dug a hole in the heap of mashed potatoes, then dropped the soggy wax beans in and covered them over. "And there's no way I'm eating this mystery meat." She cut up the cold brownish-gray hamburger and spread the pieces out. "Well, I'm done. Want me to do yours?"

"Please!" Courtney said, nibbling around the edge of the limp white bread. "This is so disgusting."

"Let's see, we don't want them to look the same." Janie began her third creation of the day.

She shoved the cut-up meat and beans together and mashed them up. "That should do. I'm getting really good at this."

Courtney watched, fascinated. "It almost looks as if someone actually tried eating it."

"Yeah, I know," Janie said, rather pleased, "but we have to figure more ways to get rid of this stuff. Maybe we could hide it in a toybox in the ward or behind some books in the waiting room. Or, how about we try the kid across the hall. He looks like he'd eat anything." She considered the three-inch square of yellow cake and jabbed it with her thumb. "Hey . . . I have an idea." She broke the bread into chunks and dumped all the crumbs into a paper napkin.

Clutching the napkin sack, she climbed up onto the sill and opened the unlatched window. "Be on the lookout for Mrs. Bicker, will ya? If she catches me doing one more number, you're going to have to work up a very quick spell. Like turning me into a bedpan."

"There's no one in the hall." Courtney poked her head out the doorway.

"Gawd, will you look at all those starving pigeons. This stuff probably won't hurt them too much."

Janie was surprised when Courtney climbed up on the ledge beside her. "That would be terrific, Janie."

The two girls stood together on top of the windowsill, looking down at the winter city. On the street, three stories below, were hundreds of gray pigeons, hunting and pecking in a narrow strip of sidewalk. Courtney agreed with Janie that most likely the birds would not be harmed by the hospital's food. Together they threw dry cake and squashy bread out into the city.

"Okay," said Janie decisively, "Now that that's done, let's go out for lunch. I've got some money my father left for emergencies."

"We can't do that. We'd get caught."

"No, we wouldn't. All we have to do is—"

"I have no desire to get in trouble." Courtney sniffed.

"Oh, come on! It's so boring around here, I even did my homework. Just think how great it will be outdoors."

"No way," Courtney was curt. "Besides it's too cold."

"Listen, suppose we just go down to the coffee shop for an ice cream cone?"

"Well, okay but, only as far as the coffee shop, and if we get caught—"

"Yeah, Courtney!" Janie jumped onto the chair and then the floor, waving her arms and hooting. "We won't get caught!"

"Now, the best way to do this," said Janie in a serious tone, "is to act very natural. If we just walk down the hall and get on the elevator as if we do it all the time, everything will be okay."

"Oh sure, people always go for ice cream

cones in pajamas." Courtney wrinkled her nose. "Don't you think someone might notice?"

Janie was surprised. She hadn't thought about details. "Well that's easy," she bluffed. "All we have to do is put on our clothes and wear bathrobes over them till we get downstairs."

"And do you expect us to just get on the elevator? If anyone is sitting in the nurses' station, she'll see us.

Janie looked up at Courtney who was still on the window ledge. Courtney was making her think about all sorts of stuff and taking the fun out of her idea. "You sure are making this hard." She began pacing between the two hospital beds. "Suppose we go down the hall in our bathrobes, as if we're going into the waiting room to use the phone." She grinned as the idea formed and became fun again. "Now, as we walk by the elevator, you hit the button so it will stop on this floor. Then, we wait in the telephone booth to see if anyone is in the elevator. If it's empty when the doors open, and the hall is clear, we can run out and ride down."

Courtney frowned. She couldn't stall any longer. The plan seemed likely to work. "Well, let's try and see how far we get. Don't forget your money," she said, stepping down gracefully.

They were going out the door in bulky bathrobes with slacks rolled up and coins silenced in pocketed handkerchiefs. "Wait!" Courtney ordered. "What are we going to do with our bathrobes after we get on the elevator, and how do we get into them again when we come back?"

"Oh, come on," Janie whined. "All I want is a crummy ice cream cone so I don't starve to death. Why are you making everything so complicated? I don't want to go if it's not any fun."

"Now, just a minute, Janie. You started this and I don't want to get in any trouble. We're going down there because now I want an ice cream cone too. All we have to do is take a paper bag with us and stuff our robes in that."

Courtney rummaged around in her nightstand and found a bag that she had brought some of her things in. "Look, Janie, this is perfect. No one will question a shopping bag."

This time they made it out the door and down the hall. When they came to the nurses' office, Courtney took a big guilty breath and kept on walking. She did not turn her head, but only looked straight. Passing obviously close to the elevator, she pushed the button before entering the phone booth.

It was then that she noticed Janie was not right behind her. Not only had Janie not followed the plan, but she had also stopped at the nurses' office. Courtney did not believe what she was hearing.

"Mrs. Bickerstaff." Janie smiled sweetly. "Would you have change for a dollar? I'd like to use the phone."

The elevator doors opened. No one stepped off or on. The doors closed again, and the light winked off. Courtney stood in the stuffy phone booth while Janie chatted with Mrs. Bickerstaff, who did not seem to notice the elevator's odd behavior.

Jingling the coins in her hand, Janie shoved into the phone booth beside Courtney. She banged the door shut before she started laughing.

"Why are you making a phone call now?" Courtney could not suppress her irritation.

"Oh," Janie chuckled, "I'm not going to call anyone now—later when I get back, or maybe tomorrow."

Courtney wished for fire-breathing dragons to take care of Janie. "What are we going to do now, Janie?"

"Well," said Janie slowly, trying to think quickly, "we are . . . not taking the elevator . . because we are . . . walking down. We can change in the stairwell and not run into anyone that way."

"Then let's get going."

Trying not to bound out of the booth, the girls began the adventure again. Down the three flights they raced, pulling robes off on the last landing. They shoved the robes in the bag, opened the exit door to a busy hall, and disappeared among the crowds of preoccupied people.

At the entrance to the gift and coffee shop, Courtney came to an abrupt stop and Janie crashed into her. Courtney grabbed Janie by the wrist and dragged her into the aisle between the cards and toys.

"Why did you do that?" Janie demanded. "I want to get—"

"Did you see who was sitting at the counter? We have to go right back upstairs this minute. It's Dr. Michaels. He's the one who saw me this morning. He'll know me, Janie!"

"Hey, come on. He sees hundreds of people a day. He won't even recognize you."

"He knows me, Janie. He's my orthopedist. He treats all the kids with scoliosis. He might even know who you are."

Janie made a face. "You think you're so special that he'll remember you out of a million other kids. Just walk up and order an ice cream and then we'll leave," Janie coaxed. "It'll be easy. He'll never notice."

"No!" Courtney would not budge out of the side aisle.

"OK. I'll go get the cones. What kind do you want?"

"Strawberry," Courtney mumbled, trying to peek over the toy display.

Janie marched up to the counter and sat on the revolving stool. She twirled around twice before ordering. "Two double scoops of strawberry ice cream with sprinkles. And we want sugar cones, too."

"Janie, did you ever hear the word please?"

Janie's jaw dropped open. Dr. Michaels winked as he fished money out of his pocket.

Then he left. She watched him go by the coffee shop window out into the hall.

"Hey, girlie, you want these cones or not? I haven't got all day!"

Still looking through the window, Janie felt in her pocket and handed over the money. Courtney emerged from hiding.

Out in the hall, Janie looked back in the shop window at the counter with the revolving stools, the shelves of candy, newspapers, and toys. The girl behind the counter was drinking a cup of coffee, smoking a cigarette, and reading the newest movie magazine. Absently, Janie handed Courtney an ice cream that had begun dripping.

They started down the nearly empty hall. "Ohh," Janie moaned, "I think I'm in love."

Courtney glanced down the long tan corridor. Dr. Michaels was getting on the elevator up ahead. "He's so handsome. I wrote in my journal that he was the vanquished king of Greno, in hiding till the red sands run black again." She sighed and bit into the sugar cone.

Janie winced. "You know what?" she said looking at the melting pink ice cream. "I don't feel so hot. Do you want this?" Her tummy had begun complaining again.

# 5

It was nearly dark out when Janie climbed back up on the windowsill with two uneaten dinners in a paper napkin. "How's it look?"

"All clear!" Courtney hoisted herself up to the ledge beside Janie.

"Bombs away," Janie yelled, letting go of a cold meatball.

"Save me some. I want to throw my own."

Janie handed over the greasy napkin and watched indulgently as Courtney threw down globs of spaghetti. "Think of it, meatballs and macaroni falling out of the sky. Wonder if pigeons like Italian food?" She laughed out loud. "Boy, this is really neat."

"I'm glad we're doing it together." Courtney's smile was deliberate.

An easy glow in Janie's eyes flashed back at Courtney. She flung her arm over the other girl's shoulders. "There might be Irish pigeons out there and Italian ones. Think of it, Cass, we'll have to throw out all kinds of food to be fair."

Janie felt a stiffness rise in Courtney's shoulders. She had made a terrible slip.

Courtney didn't answer. With one hand still extended out the window, she watched the oily napkin flapping against the glass pane. But her mind seemed to be concentrating on something very far away.

Frantically Janie groped for something to say. "Sure looks cold out there, doesn't it?" Courtney's silence made her uncomfortable.

"You know what, Janie," Courtney whispered, "I almost can't believe it . . . you just summoned my hidden name. That means we're bound to each other in friendship forever. How did you guess?"

Janie's eyes traced the outline of the buildings, all different shapes and sizes, against the black cloudless sky. The full moon gave everything it touched an eerie silver glow. She noticed the wind howling somewhere out there. Trapped in an alley, she thought, racing up and down with no way to get out.

"Oh, Janie, that's so fantastic! It never happened with anyone else before, and I've always wanted it to. Last night I wasn't sure, but after today. . . ." Courtney rambled on excitedly.

The knot in Janie's stomach, the one that had been there all day, tightened. Pressing herself against the glass, she felt its coolness through her robe and pajamas.

I don't want to, Janie thought, gripping the window sash with both hands. I don't want to. She closed her eyes and shook her head. A jabbing pain ran up to her chest—it would not be ignored.

"Please tell me how you did it. Maybe you have very strong magical powers, and you don't even know it. In Greno. . . ."

Janie bit her lip and shook her head. "No," she said, "no, I didn't . . . guess . . . I. . . ."

"But you did. You just said it," Courtney insisted. "How else would you have known but by magic. I never told anyone or even said it out loud. The only place that I've used it is in my. . . ."

"I. . . ."

"Janie?"

"Yeah, I. . . ."

"Janie, you read my diary?" Courtney's eyes were wide and fierce with disbelief. "You were lying this morning! And when you said about that lady, I believed you."

"But that was true. She really did—"

"Oh, sure, I bet! What a little creep you are. And I thought we were going to be friends. I should have known not to trust you when you couldn't keep your mouth shut about the bridge."

"What do you mean?" Janie asked, rubbing her nagging stomach.

"I had never told anyone about that bridge. I didn't want the whole world to know. But you didn't care about that."

"But it was such a beautiful idea. Why should it be a secret?"

"It just was. Like my name," Courtney said, letting go of the napkin. The wind grabbed it up and hurled it against the night.

Awkwardly, Courtney turned, sat down on the ledge and slipped off. Leaving the room, she snatched the diary. "And when my parents get here tomorrow . . ."

Janie jumped feet first from the window, unable to hear the last of the threat. Not knowing if she felt better or worse, she dashed into the hall. "Hey, Courtney, wait up a sec . . . Courtney?"

The corridor was deserted. As Janie decided to head up the hall instead of down, she was only vaguely aware of the after-dinner hush. It was the silence of a day almost completed, when the staff attended to bedding down the youngest children. There were a few muffled cries and complaints from the Babies Ward, but mostly it was a whispering time. Only the indifferent wind went on screeching.

Janie followed the green paint stripe on the wall, down the dimly lit corridor, around the corner, and through the waiting room. There was only one place to hide. She opened the fire door.

"Courtney-Ann? Are you out here?" There was no response.

Leaning over the banister, Janie peered down the stairwell. "Come on, Courtney, I know you're here." She listened to the silence.

The faintest overhead sound sent Janie up the stairs two at a time. On the fifth-floor landing Janie found Courtney huddled up.

"Go away and leave me alone." She kept her face in her hands.

"Listen, Courtney, I'm sorry." Janie sat down next to her. "I really am. I mean it. I never did anything like that before. I don't even know why I read it. I guess I wanted to find out about you."

Courtney slid down to the next stair and over closer to the wall. Janie moved down and over with her.

"Will you please leave me alone!"

"No!"

"Well, I'm never talking to you again."

"You can't do that. That's so—" Janie stopped herself from making the situation even worse. She sat chin in hand gazing down at the huge red number five painted on the landing wall. Why would anyone paint an eight-foot numeral? That was pretty stupid, almost as stupid as. . . .

"What part did you read?" Courtney demanded abruptly.

"Just what you wrote yesterday, about wanting to be friends."

"Nothing else?"

"Nope."

Courtney turned her frowning face and accusing eyes toward Janie. She said nothing.

"Honest!"

Janie thought she saw some of the anger in Courtney's face clear, but she wasn't sure. Janie also noticed that for the first time since she'd read the diary, her stomach seemed to be quiet.

"Courtney, what could I do to make you stop being angry at me?"

"Nothing. I'll never forgive you. What you did was bad."

Janie cringed under the harshness of Courtney's words. But she went on trying to think of something. "In Greno, when someone is bad, what happens?"

"Quit making fun of Greno, will you? You think it's stupid, so just cut it out!"

"No, it isn't stupid. I told you that last night. And I mean it. What do they do in Greno?"

Courtney glared at Janie, her eyes lit with suspicion. "They are very kind in Greno. They never punish people. They just have the person who made the mistake give back what she's taken or do a task that will blot out the evil. It's always balanced out fairly."

"Then think of something that I can do for you."

"Why don't you go jump off that bridge." Even as she made her sarcastic remark, Courtney wondered if she could be as forgiving and noble as the wronged Princess Suskayha. If she really believed in Greno, then what Janie asked had to be completed. It was the way of the Grens.

"Oh, come on, Courtney," Janie begged.

"All you'd have to do to make things even," Courtney said reluctantly, "is tell me your deepest secret and your hidden name. That is, if you have such things!"

Janie knew she had plenty of secrets! She didn't know which would be the most difficult to tell Courtney. There was the one about the time she and Harold tried smoking out in the woods. The cigars had made her sick. And once she had taken care of Diane, the class beauty and the class snob. She'd left a basket of freshly dug-up worms on Diane's front stoop after school. That was pretty awful, but it had also been funny watching Diane answer the doorbell, from Harold's bedroom window.

"Hey, Courtney, I do have a name that I could tell you. It's my real one instead of a fantasy name. And I hate it so much, I never use it."

"I thought it was Janie."

"No, that's my nickname. This name doesn't fit me at all."

"Okay." Courtney was slightly intrigued. "Tell me."

"You have to promise you'll never tell. I don't want anyone to know."

"If you won't tell my magical name, then I won't use your real one. But do you promise?"

"Yup," said Janie, enthusiastically.

"How do I know that I can trust you now?" Courtney's question was blunt.

Janie felt as though she'd been punched in her unhappy stomach, but she forced herself to keep trying. "Well," she said after a while, "at home when my father wants to know the truth about something, he says a special word. 'Teddy Bear.' And I know when he uses it that no matter what's happened or what's been said, I have to tell the truth. He says that feeling able to tell the truth is really the important thing. So, Teddy Bear, I won't use your name if you don't use mine."

"Okay, Teddy Bear," Courtney agreed reluctantly, now that the anger and hurt were beginning to die away.

"There's one more thing that goes along with saying Teddy Bear."

"What's that?"

"Well," Janie said shyly, "we have to give each other bear hugs, which seals it. Okay?"

Courtney thought it was a perfect idea. And just as Janie slipped her arm over Courtney's shoulder, the Arch-Queen of Greno tucked her arm around Janie's waist. "Tell me," Courtney said, gently squeezing Janie.

Janie took a deep breath. This was going to be harder than she had thought, but at least her stomach had stopped grumbling for the moment. "My real name is . . ." She paused. ". . . is Janice . . . Tannenbaum." Janie twisted up her face with her eyes tightly closed as if expecting a balloon to explode or Courtney to laugh.

"Janie, that's a beautiful name. Why don't you like it? I can't understand."

Janie fidgeted with her bathrobe tie. "I'm named after an aunt of mine who died a long time ago. She was very beautiful. Her thick blond hair hung to her waist like yours. She modeled and wanted to be a ballet dancer. I don't look anything like her photographs, with my kinky hair and orange freckles. My mother says she was good in sports like me, but I don't think I'll be like her when I grow up."

Courtney understood. And, she thought, Janie had more than made up for reading her diary. "Janie," she said, "I like how you look, especially your nose. I think Janice is a beautiful name, but I like calling you Janie. Janice sounds too grown-up; maybe that's why it doesn't seem to fit."

Janie shrugged, still embarrassed. But when Courtney hugged her again, Janie knew that what her father had said about never taking no for an answer was true.

For a while they were quiet and then they talked, drifting in and out of conversation like old friends often do when they find there are still things they don't know about one another. Janie was telling Courtney about the spitball war she had organized in school.

"We've been here one day. It seems like weeks already."

"I know," Janie agreed. "So much gets squashed into the time."

When the door opened two flights below, both Janie and Courtney had a feeling it was Ms. Rogers looking for them. They peered over the railing at the stiff white cap that rested on her black hair.

"I think she's the most beautiful lady I've ever seen," Janie whispered.

"Me too."

"Hey, Ms. Rogers," Janie's yell bounced off the walls. "We're up here."

"Listen, you two, you can't keep disappearing. The volunteer who does arts and crafts at night has been frantic looking for you."

"Okay, we're coming." Janie stood up.

When they reached the landing with the gigantic red three, Janie could tell that Ms. Rogers was not really annoyed with them. "You should at least tell me where you're going," she said, trying to be stern.

Janie opened the door. Bracing herself against it, she waited for Ms. Rogers and Courtney.

"Janie and I had something to discuss,"

Courtney explained in a very assured manner. "We needed to have some privacy."

Ms. Rogers nodded her head. "That's fine with me, but I still must know where you are at all times."

"We'll make a point of it, Ms. Rogers," Courtney said confidently. Then she winked at Janie as she and the nurse passed through the doorway.

What next? Janie thought, dumbfounded by Courtney. And this was only day one. "Boy, would I ever like something good to eat," she said a bit too loudly in the empty hall.

"There's some chocolate milk and graham crackers in your room," Ms. Rogers whispered. "Good night."

# 6

Janie skidded through the door of 318K so fast that her sneakers made black marks on the brown linoleum floor. When she saw the doctors clustered around Courtney's bed, she stuck out her tongue at their backs. Why, Janie wondered, did they have to be there, now of all times, when she had something really important to tell Courtney? Doctors' rounds, thought Janie, annoyed by the daily intrusion. These guys came around to the rooms talking about the patients as if they weren't even there, checking this one's stitches and that one's leg. What a pain!

Janie banged her feet against the metal rails of the hospital bed. Her sneakers made a dull thudding sound. One of the interns glanced over her shoulder at Janie. Dr. Michaels frowned at her without stopping his explanation of the body cast that Courtney would be going into.

Janie got the message. "Boy," she griped. "Can't do a thing around here." She jumped off the bed and marched around the end of it. Crouching down, she began pumping up the head of the bed with the hand crank. She didn't even bother to watch how far up it rose before she began cranking the foot end. When the handle could go no further, Janie stood. The mattress was all but folded in half.

"Wow, will you look at that? Fan-tas-tic!"

Janie climbed into the hollow of the bed, adjusted the pillow halfway up the mattress, and leaned against it with her shoulder. Then she swung her legs around and lifted them up against the other half of the not-quite-doubled bed. Her knees were level with her face. She giggled as she traced the wrinkle and stain designs in her hospital pajamas.

"Are you quite comfortable?" Dr. Michaels asked. "It looks like a rather inconvenient position."

"Oh, yes, very," responded Janie in her best adult imitation. "I often sit like this when my back is bothering me."

"Really?" The doctor nodded, stroking his chin. The corners of his mouth fought down a smile. "And you find it helps?"

Janie knew he was teasing. "Ah, yes. I would recommend it to all of your patients."

Behind Dr. Michaels some of the newer doctors murmured among themselves. "Well, Janie, thank you for the information. We'll be in tomorrow about the same time. Will you be available?"

"Ah . . . yes," said Janie, stroking her chin. "I'm sure I can fit it in even though I'm rather busy on Wednesdays."

Dr. Michaels smiled. "Good," he said. He and the flock of white-coated residents turned and departed.

Neat-o, Janie thought, getting out of the uncomfortable position and cranking the bed back into a more normal position. Now what was I doing? Oh, yeah.

"Hey, Courtney! You'll never believe what I saw! There's a kid down the hall with a huge body cast. You should see it! It goes from her head down to her knees. It's really something else. She looks sort of like an astronaut, without sleeves and in shorts. It's great. Lots of people signed it, and when they take it off she's going to save hunks to give to her friends. She said if we wanted we could write on it; there's still some room left on the stomach. Want to go see?"

"Is that why you came charging in here?"

"Yup."

"Where is she?"

"Just a couple of doors down. Come on. I'll show you."

"I don't think I want to right now. Maybe later."

"What's the matter? You look kind of funny." Janie crossed the small space between the two beds. She stood at the foot of Courtney's bed and looked at her friend sitting there, with feet tucked under her.

"Are you scared to see the cast?"

The princess's lips formed a pouting frown. "Janie, I . . . I know I have to go in soon, but I don't want to see it yet. Is that being a baby?"

"Yup," said Janie, "a big baby."

The frown on Courtney's face changed suddenly. "How big a baby?"

Janie cackled. "Come on. It's not so bad. Her name is Linda."

But before they could go anywhere, Mrs. Bickerstaff appeared in the doorway. Striding across the room and closing the drapes with one firm yank on the cord, she announced "Naptime!"

Janie was about to complain, but said instead, "Now, why didn't I think of that! It sounds like a wonderful idea." She stretched out on her bed and tried to yawn.

Mrs. Bickerstaff turned on her. "And I don't want to hear a sound out of this room."

When the nurse was gone, Janie whispered, "Do you think she ever says anything nice?"

Courtney's "Never," was interrupted by Mrs. Bickerstaff standing in the doorway again, hands on hips, her full chest heaving. Courtney felt guilty and Janie scared.

"I said 'no talking,' and I mean NO TALKING."

"Yes, Mrs. Bickerstaff," the girls said in chorus. The nurse rotated on the heel of her white oxford and went into the hall.

Janie was making hand signals to Courtney when she heard Mrs. Bickerstaff outside the door. "What do you mean you don't know?" the nurse demanded.

"But I don't know where it is!" Miss Parker pleaded.

"A thing that size, as big as a refrigerator, doesn't just walk away," snapped the head nurse sternly.

"I've looked everywhere I could think of, Mrs. Bickerstaff. It's just not around."

"Now, see here, young lady, I told you to find it. Immediately! And don't hand me any excuses. A mobile toilet does not vanish into thin air. Someone had to wheel it someplace."

"Yes, Mrs. Bickerstaff. I know, Mrs. Bickerstaff; but do you think someone might have taken it?"

"I certainly hope not, for their sake," Mrs. Bickerstaff said, looking over her shoulder into Room 318K. Janie's snore ended in a long thin whistle. "That person would be in a great deal of trouble. Now go find it. They need it down in the ward. I'm going back to my office and call the east wing to see if it was taken over. . . ." Her voice trailed off as she headed toward her office.

Janie and Courtney looked at each other from

their beds. "Wait till she gets there." Janie tried to whisper.

"What do you mean?"

"The thing is in her office, with that green plastic rubber tree from the waiting room sitting inside the bowl. She'll blow a gasket!" Janie roared.

"Oh, Janie, you didn't!"

"I knew there was something else I wanted to tell you."


Courtney drifted up from a dreamless sleep. Her tensed body and rigid arms were wrapped around the pillow as if it were her old pillow-buddy at home. Though she was deeply burrowed in blankets, she felt chilled.

Unbending her legs, Courtney eased them away from the warm spots she had made between the sheets. She unclenched one fist and studied the red fingernail marks in her palm.

Her eyes leaped from the open hand to the window. They ran up, across, down, and over each of the wood-framed glass panes. There were three panes up, four across, or one, two, three, four, five, six, seven, eight, nine, ten, eleven, twelve—or three times four, or four times three. Her eyes fingered the squares again and again, noticing the dried paint droplets that would never dribble down the glass.

Even though it was warm in the room, Courtney felt a cold within that matched the wind outside. She shuddered, pulling the blankets up, and rolled over, making a tight cocoon.

"Courtney." A whisper reached across the semi-darkness. "Are you napping?" Janie was wide awake.

"No. I thought you were."

"Nope. I can't sleep. The wind's so awful."

"I know, it sounds like a dragon crying because his foot is caught in a huge metal trap."

"You always have such great stories in your head. I almost could feel sorry for a dragon who was in pain."

"I've been lying here pretending to myself I was asleep and couldn't hear it."

"Why?"

"There's something about the wind that makes being in the hospital even scarier. I don't know why, but it's even worse when it's dark out and the wind goes howling."

Janie agreed. "Are you scared about the cast? I can't imagine not being able to get out of bed for a long time."

Courtney sighed. "I know." The tears flooded her eyes and her throat tightened. "Oh, Janie, I wish we really had run away the other day. I don't want this. Why can't I be home going to school like my friends? Why did this have to happen to me? I don't want to be different from other kids. It's not fair. I hate it." The tears dripped down Courtney's face. "I wish there would be a volcano or an earthquake."

"What do you mean?"

"Well, if the building split in half, then they couldn't put casts on us and we would probably get to go home even."

"Sure," mused Janie, enjoying the thought of the building cracking open like a nut. "But you know what? There's lots of sick people here. It wouldn't be fair to them."

"I know."

"And besides you're not the only one. It's happening to me, too. At least we're here at the same time. It won't be as bad as you think. My mother always says stuff like that, and most of the time she's right."

"Sometimes I can't help feeling bad."

"Me too." Janie stayed awake after Courtney's breathing relaxed into sleep.

In the hall a child cried for her squeaky toy train, the intercom demanded a Dr. Ross report to surgery and a student nurse pushed a wheelchair into a patient's room. Outside in the late winter cold, the dragon sharpened his claws against the building.

# 7

---

It was a windy dawn when a nurse Courtney
had never seen before leaned over her bed. Not
Ms. Rogers, her favorite nurse, this lady told
Courtney to get out of bed and into the wheelchair quickly.

Courtney did not look out the window as she
slid into the chair. She knew the dragon who
had been there yesterday and all through the
night was still restless. He kept throwing himself against the building and raking the frozen
ground with his jagged tail.

"Where are we going?" she asked.

"Shuush."

"Can Janie come with us?"

"No," was the nurse's only reply as she
wheeled Courtney down the hall.

Waiting for the elevator, Courtney studied the unfamiliar face. It was not old, but the mouth turned down into a frown that looked permanently etched. The nurse's thin hair was parted on one side and wrenched into a stiff knot behind her little ears. A long pinched nose sat above a large square chin. Courtney pretended in the glow of the red exit light that the lady was a witch. She didn't have any warts, though.

On the elevator the nurse pushed the button T, and the doors slid together soundlessly. "What does T stand for?" asked Courtney.

"The tunnel. We are going through the tunnel and into another building."

"Tunnel! What tunnel?" Courtney, now wide awake, was curious and a bit scared. Where was this strange nurse taking her? What was in the other building?

The numbers flashed above the elevator doors. Three! There was something about this she did not like. Two! It reminded her of something she had once read. One! It was the fairy tale about the spring maiden who was fed to the dragon-headed dog. Basement! She didn't even know till she got there! Tunnel THE TUNNEL! THE DRAGON! Maybe that was it, thought Courtney, only half believing her own game. The witch dressed in nurse's clothing was the wicked keeper of the dog with three horns, and she, Courtney, was being taken as the sacrifice! Wait till she told Janie!

The elevator doors opened. A cold draft rushed in and splashed against the doomed maiden. The lights of the elevator flashed into the darkness ahead as they rattled into the moldy-smelling tunnel. The doors closed, and, the elevator climbed away to safety. Light bulbs studded the long damp ceiling and water stains covered the cracked concrete walls.

Up ahead something was slowly making its way closer to them as she was being pushed toward it. A man, hunched to one side, began to appear. Straight gray hair hung down to his sloping shoulders. Long arms dangled around his bent legs. Swaying, he dragged his twisted body.

The evil sorcerer! Courtney shivered as his face took on a shape. Slowly he crept nearer. She shut her eyes expecting his awful magic.

When the dragon dog did not strike, she opened her eyes again. A tired face, more scared than her own, hesitated before Courtney. An old man, she thought. She smiled deliberately and his wrinkled face lit up. The sad blue eyes sparkled.

They passed each other, locked in a silent friendship. Then she heard him shuffling back into the darkness. From now on, Courtney decided, she'd try smiling at monsters and dragons to make them disappear.

At the end of the tunnel they climbed a ramp and turned a corner. "Where are we going?"

Courtney asked again, guessing the answer even before the nurse spoke.

"We are outfitting you with your cast this morning, Courtney."

Courtney closed her eyes when the lady in a green hospital gown began snipping. She heard the shears chewing at her hair and felt the slippery locks fall away from her ear. A sob broke loose, and tears brimmed up between thick blond lashes.

No! Courtney buried the scream. No! This couldn't be happening. Princess Suskayha, she pleaded, command the Snail Masters to rise up again. They just had to take her away from this dungeon. The maiden's tears flowed from a bottomless well of fear.

The lady in the green skullcap stepped around the front end of the high metal table. "It's hard, I know. You have such beautiful hair." Her voice was gentle.

"No one told me my hair had to be cut," Courtney murmured.

"Oh, sweetie, that was a slip-up. Somebody goofed. I thought you knew." She put the shears down.

Courtney shook her head. "Not till a second ago when I saw the scissors."

"I'm sorry."

"Does it have to be cut?"

"Yes," she said simply.

"But why?"

"Because the cast goes over the top of your head. Your hair would get all full of wet plaster even if we braided it."

Suskayha, Courtney pleaded. The mythical princess of Greno remained silent. "All right," Courtney said after a while. "I understand. But could I ask a favor—no, two favors?

The nameless woman nodded. "Tell me."

"Would you make one long braid and cut it off quickly? And could you get Janie, the girl in my room, to keep me company? I'm not very brave, and she is. If she were here, I'd feel better."

The lady turned away, then stopped and came back. She took Courtney's face between her soft hands and stared at her. "I must tell you that you're mistaken. You're a very brave girl, even though you may not feel as if it's true."

For the first time Courtney noticed the woman's eyes. They were the exact color gray as all the creatures of Greno. There was something comforting in that.

"Now, let me see what I can do."

While Courtney waited for the woman to get off the phone, she stared about the unfriendly white room. There were all sorts of fierce metal instruments hanging on the tile walls and lying on the tables. It looked like a torture chamber more than a hospital. Her momentary courage faltered. Courtney wished that she really were brave.

The lady put the receiver down and opened a white cabinet door. "She's on her way."

"Thank you," Courtney said.

"It's quite all right. It's the very least I can do." She handed Courtney a paper cup and a small pill. "Here, I want you to take this. It will help to relax you a bit. And I'll tell you what's going to happen this morning while we're waiting. Let me braid your hair as I'm talking. Over there is a pile of felt, newspapers, and gauze. The first thing. . . ."

Courtney drank all the water. She took a deep breath and tried to pay attention. It was important to listen, but she kept thinking that any moment Janie would arrive. It was so weird that two days ago she and Janie had been enemies and now she couldn't wait for Janie to get here.

"The cast has several layers. . . ." the lady was saying when Janie's wheelchair came through the swinging wooden doors like a bulldozer.

"Hey you guys, what's going on? This isn't the barber shop, it's a hospital. Why are you cutting her hair?"

"It's no use, Janie. They have to, because of the cast."

Janie slouched in her wheelchair. Very slowly she twirled around, taking in the room. "Are you sure?" She halted.

Courtney nodded. She was getting sleepy.

"Well, look who I brought. I thought you might use your magical powers." Janie heaved the leather beanbag frog at Courtney.

"Oh, Janie," Courtney rubbed her face against the frog's suede belly. "Greno doesn't work anymore. It's all gone."

"Baloney," Janie jumped up. She stood between Courtney's legs, looking up into her face. "And don't say that . . . you know it's just this creepy place. Hey . . . you're going to look really neat with short hair.

The scissors clattered onto the steel table. The woman was done. Courtney shook her head, unconvinced, the tears welling up again.

"Courtney," Janie pleaded, "Teddy Bear!"

Courtney began sobbing. "Janie, I don't want this."

Janie understood. She didn't want it either. But there was nothing she could do, or anyone else, to make it different.

Courtney slid off the end of the table. She stumbled toward Janie. "Give me a hug." Her voice was drowsy.

"It's okay, Courtney," Janie whispered. "Keep thinking Greno, and I'll see you later."

The lady in green slipped a supporting arm around Courtney. "Come lie down now."

Thrusting her freckled hands deep into her pockets, Janie turned away. The floor was strewn with hair. An orderly was already sweeping it toward the garbage can. Janie grabbed up the long yellow braid. Spun gold, she thought sadly.

She glanced back just before the wooden door swung closed. Courtney was lying sedated on a metal table with little wisps of blond hair sticking up all around her head. Her profile seemed vulnerable and naked. Janie wished that they had hung her hair out the window, just like what's-her-face in the tower. Then they could have climbed down and run away. She fingered the long silky braid in her pocket as the nurse pushed the wheelchair back down the hall and through the tunnel.

# 8

Janie couldn't get away from the panic. It kept grabbing her. No matter what she had done all day, it had been there like a dragon clawing her. She fingered the braid inside her pocket. Now she knew what Courtney had been feeling this morning.

"No! I will not cry! I am not a baby," Janie told herself for the hundredth time. She bounded out of a waiting room chair, through the fire exit door and onto the landing.

Only the view from the second story window made her stop running. This was the place she and Courtney had talked about Greno on the very first night.

Outside in the late afternoon darkness the

lights on the bridge twinkled. Just like diamonds. It did look like a necklace. Greno was real and not real all at the same time. Now, she understood it.

She closed her eyes and opened her mouth the way she'd seen Courtney do. Greno—Janie addressed the magical realm inside her head—would you do something for me? I'm Janie, Courtney's friend. I just heard about you the other day. Could you take the pounding noise out of my head? And keep me from crying? I don't want to cry. I'm too old for that baby stuff. "Thanks," she said aloud.

She waited, thinking it might be worth a try. But nothing happened, no enchanted visions or lightning striking. "Oh, well." She shrugged her shoulders. "I just thought I'd ask."

She studied the birds huddled together on the sidewalk. Janie wondered what it was like to be a pigeon and peck food from the dirt. It was a good thing she'd thought of feeding them. This was probably the worst part of the pigeons' year, the winter almost over and nothing growing yet. They ought to have some birdseed, like Harold put out on his back porch.

Harold! Harold seemed like a dream she had had once. And only a couple of days had gone by!

Somebody opened the landing door at the top of the stairs. "I don't care who it is," Janie muttered. Let them yell at me, she thought, for not being in that room. She listened to the footsteps coming down the stairs. They stopped behind her.

"Hello, Janie."

She turned around. "Dr. Michaels?"

"I was just in your room."

"Is Courtney back?"

"Yes."

"Is she okay?"

"She's fine. A bit sleepy."

"Is she in pain?"

"No, maybe a little uncomfortable. It takes some getting used to."

From nowhere the dragon lashed out. "Dr. Michaels." Janie gulped. "I don't think . . . I mean . . ." She struggled. "How will . . . I ever . . . live inside that thing? I can't even stay in bed when I have a cold. The tears broke loose as the doctor reached out.

Janie sobbed and sobbed. Her face against his stomach felt the starchy clean smock and the hard white button pressing into her forehead.

The doctor's hands, holding the sides of her throbbing head, were cool. That would keep her brains from exploding, she thought. He let her go on weeping till no tears were left.

Looking down at the tips of his brown leather boots, Janie said, "I didn't know I was such a scaredy cat."

"There are times when crying is good for you. I cry once in a while. And I don't think it has anything to do with being cowardly."

Janie looked up. She wasn't sure what surprised her the most.

"You can be brave and frightened all at the same time. Maybe, you're even braver if you let yourself cry."

Janie took a big deep breath. "You think so?" It certainly helped to know you didn't get kicked out of being brave if you cried.

The doctor nodded, his gray eyes reassuring. "Yes, I do. Why don't you go back to your room. I bet Courtney would like some company."

"Okay."

"And don't worry, Janie. It won't be too bad."

"You know what, Dr. Michaels? I sort of made this wish on Courtney's bridge"—Janie looked out the window with him—"and it came true. Thanks."

"Good," said the doctor. "I'm glad."

Janie turned to leave. "Will my hair be cut too?"

"No, I don't think so."

"Why not?" Janie put her hands on her hips. "Courtney's was. Why can't mine be?"

"It's really not too long. Do you want to have it clipped?"

"Yes," said Janie, "definitely. I want the exact same hair style as Courtney."

"Well, in that case"—Dr. Michaels chuckled —"we'll make sure you have a trim!" He headed down the stairs.

Taking one last look at the necklace-bridge that would not be seen for months, Janie beck-

oned in her own way. Nice work, Greno, whoever or whatever you are. "Ah-bee-sin-eyah!"
She took the stairs two at a time

The fan clicked off when Janie stepped out of
the phone booth and into the waiting room. She
stopped to snap every handle on the candy machine just because she was feeling like her old
self. Her parents said they'd be there tomorrow
with a special surprise. And her mother had
said that the kids at school had put a huge package in the mail.

Janie scooted around the corner and down
the hall. " 'Lo there, Miss Parker," she called out
to the open utility cabinet where the nurse was
down on her hands and knees searching for
something. Miss Parker's response was muffled.
And Janie kept right on going.

Calling Harold again had been a good idea
also. He'd written down every word of the
grafitti and come up with the idea of sending
birdseed for the pigeons. Janie laughed, thinking of Harold saying that he'd figure out a fool-
proof way of slipping the stuff into the hospital
right under the authorities' noses. There were
always AUTHORITIES, he had told her. Janie wasn't
sure if this hospital had any. She just did not
want Mrs. Bicker to find out.

Janie laughed some more. If she had to marry
someday, she guessed it might as well be Harold. She was wondering where such junky

thoughts came from when she entered her room. She stopped short—jolted by the harsh reality of the huge white mass partially covered with a sheet. "Courtney, is that you?"

There was no response as Janie tiptoed across the room and around the bed. Surrounded by plaster, Courtney was propped against large brown bolsters, resting on her side. Her eyes were closed.

Janie slid her palm over the surface of the cast. It was clammy and cold in a few spots but mostly it had hardened like a rough cement wall.

"Oh, Courtney. . . ." Janie closed her eyes and gritted her teeth.

"Wouldn't my friends at school be jealous of my new haircut and pretty outfit?"

"You okay?" Janie didn't know what else to say.

"Yes, but I'm so tired."

"Go back to sleep. You're not missing anything. That's for sure."

Courtney was still smiling even after she had fallen back to sleep. Perched on the windowsill, Janie studied the ugly white cast. It ran from Courtney's head to below her waist. Her arms hung out of the plaster like broken bird wings. There were also bars along each side. Janie couldn't imagine what they were for.

Janie wished she had her paint set now. She thought about covering the cast with beautiful flowers, all pinks and oranges, and making zebra stripes on the handlebars. Or maybe red would be better. They would look like candy canes, then.

Better still, she'd tell that twitchy arts and crafts volunteer, who kept bugging her to do a project, that she wanted to borrow some paint tubes. But Janie didn't move. Instead, she sat hunched on the sill, stroking the braid buried deep in her bathrobe pocket.

In the next room, a boy with his legs in traction rattled the side rails on his bed and yelled for the nurse. Janie sighed, looking down at Courtney, then out at the night sky. She was keeping watch, holding the dragon at bay.

# 9

Courtney's mother arrived a few minutes late. Usually she was on time.

"I had trouble finding a parking space and then I had to hike up that long hill. How are you doing today?"

"I'm okay. How are you?" Courtney asked politely, though she knew by looking. These days her mother was often frazzled and tired.

"I'm fine, just fine. Did you eat anything today? I brought some fruit, but you should be eating what they give you."

Courtney made a face. "There were string beans with butter for lunch. They were almost decent. Miss Parker tried to get me seconds, but she couldn't."

"That's good. Please eat. You know I worry." Mrs. Schaeffer relaxed back into the chair and looked around the room. "Where's Janie? I thought it seemed quiet!"

"She's having her cast put on. She's been gone all day. I didn't even see her this morning when she left. Janie promised to say goodbye but she didn't, so I guess the same witchy lady came for her as me."

"Courtney!" There was a warning tone in her mother's voice.

"Well, can I help it?"

"Courtney-Ann, how many times must I tell you it's not nice to say things about people."

"But, Mommy, I can't help it if that's what she looked like. Besides I didn't mean anything bad."

"I don't understand what's gotten into you lately. You were never fresh like that before."

"I just never said it out loud to anyone."

The conversation went no further. Mrs. Bickerstaff appeared. She was her usual crisp and dry self.

"Did you have a BM today?" she asked, making notations on the chart.

Courtney looked up at her and frowned. She glanced at her mother for help. "What's a BM? I never heard of it."

"It's a bowel movement," the nurse said, drawing herself up, "and it's very important, now that you're in a cast, that I know each day."

"Oh," said Courtney. "No, I didn't."

"Make sure you do before the day's out," Mrs. Bickerstaff said, before stalking off.

"Talk about witches," Courtney mumbled. She almost didn't care if her mother heard.

"I brought you something," Mrs. Schaeffer said, reaching for her bag.

Out of her brown purse, which always seemed like a little bit of home to Courtney, Mrs. Schaeffer took a bright package wrapped in tissue paper. "I didn't have time to fix this up pretty for you. And I was so excited, I couldn't wait till tomorrow to bring it."

Courtney unfolded the layers of magenta tissue. When it was finally unraveled, a tiny pewter castle rested on her hand.

It had four lookout turrets with little windows and a tower in the middle. There was a walkway around the inside edge and even an archway that led out to a moat. The inside was hollowed out and Courtney fit the entire castle on her second finger like a large thimble. She closed her hand around it.

"Oh, Mommy, it's beautiful. I never saw such a thing, but I think I've always wanted it. It's perfect!"

"I thought so too." Her mother glowed. She bent over the bed to kiss her daughter on the cheek.

It was then that the commotion began in the hall. They were both startled. It sounded like a gang of Christmas carolers had been let loose in the middle of March.

The stretcher table with Janie in her cast came through the door, head first. Janie singing, "O Tannenbaum, O Tannenbaum," at the top of her lungs, was accompanied by the orderly, maneuvering the table. His rich baritone voice rang out above three generations of Tannenbaum harmony. And at the rear end of the table, though no one paid any attention, Mrs. Bickerstaff was fuming and sputtering about the noise.

"Well, I guess Janie's back," Courtney said to her mother.

"Hi," Janie bellowed. "How's it going, turtle twin?"

Courtney smiled. "Fine, Janie. How are you?"

"Super! Guess what? That's my grandmother. She came all the way from Florida to see me."

"O Tannenbaum, O Tannenbaum," the family began again, and Janie's grandmother took a bow with the orderly.

It was Courtney who noticed Dr. Michaels standing in the doorway. He didn't look like a doctor, dressed in a reddish brown leather jacket and black slacks. And the gray cashmere sweater was the exact color of his eyes. Courtney blushed when he stepped into the room. She couldn't say a word.

Janie stopped singing when she saw him, also surprised, but the adults went on. They hadn't noticed him.

"Dr. Michaels!" Janie yelped.

There was an abrupt silence in the room. Everyone felt foolish.

"Oh, no no, please don't stop. I had to check someone else on the floor so I decided to see how my two friends were doing. I heard the singing out in the hall, and I knew everything was all right. See you in a few days." He knocked on Janie's new cast and left.

Mrs. Bickerstaff took advantage of the momentary lull. "Visiting hours are over for today," she announced. "Everyone will have to leave immediately."

Five minutes later Janie and Courtney were alone in a room that had suddenly grown very large. What had been a few steps between beds might as well have been the other side of the world, now.

Janie cupped her hands around her mouth and made her voice quaver. "Earth to Courtney. Come in, please."

Courtney giggled. "You have reached the Arch-Queen of the planet Greno. Bespeak your request."

By the time the dinner trays arrived, they were roaring with laughter. "I think my parents brought some food we can have instead of this junk." Janie opened the brown paper bag on the bed and stuck her nose in.

"There's lots of good stuff here, Courtney. Bagels with cream cheese, and my grandmother's mandel bread. You'll love it. "Hey, what's this?" Janie said, unwrapping a bulky package. "Birdseed! Harold!" she whooped, "you did it."

"Take it away, Mabel," Janie commanded as the little white-haired volunteer pushed the library cart out of the room.

"Why'd you ask for the Bible? There were all kinds of good things on the truck," Courtney said, leafing through a slick magazine called, *Love Affairs*.

"Nothing else looked too hot to me. Maybe I can find the dirty parts in the Bible. I heard it had some."

"You're kidding!"

"Nope!" Janie flipped through the leather-bound volume without a clear cut idea of what she was looking for. After a while she thumped it closed. "I give up. Maybe tomorrow."

"Want to read one of my books about Greno?"

"Hey, yeah! That would be neat."

"I have the first book about a girl with wings and a boy who rode upon a snail. It's really good."

"Sounds pretty kinky. Let me see it."

But the glance they exchanged admitted that there was absolutely no way for Courtney to hand the book to Janie. Each was bound within a shell, immobile and untouchable.

"That's the pits," Janie groaned. She punched

the bolster underneath her cast, which tilted her up slightly into a kneeling position.

Courtney's hand felt around the bed for the flasher on a cord. When she clicked it on, the light outside their door began blinking.

"Don't get upset, Janie," she said gently. "One of the nurses will give it to you."

Janie stretched her arm over toward the one-legged table beside her bed. The remote control for the television was also beyond her finger tips. "Damn it all," Janie muttered under her breath. "If I could just move a little."

Janie pressed her body against the inside of the cast. It was like leaning against a cave, only she was wearing the walls. Just her arms and lower legs were free.

And there was no way to roll over either. The bars along the sides of the cast, she discovered, were for the nurses to flip her onto her back. And being in that position reminded Janie of insects, helplessly struggling to get right side up. She used to think it was funny to watch bugs on their backs with their legs thrashing. But now, she promised herself, she'd never torment them again.

Flattening her hands wide open on the mattress, Janie pushed her body against the top of the cast. The muscles under her arms strained. She pushed harder. The thing lifted away from the bolster. Very slowly and very unsteadily Janie rose, supporting herself on her arms.

"Courtney, look what I can do," Janie said, not daring to take her eyes off her arms.

"Janie! Be careful! You might be doing something terrible to your spine."

"I don't think so. All the weight is in my arms." Janie lowered herself to relieve the aching muscles. "Wow, that's terrific. Why don't you try it?"

"I'm too scared."

The second time Janie lifted her head and looked around. "I can even see out the window, Courtney." Janie stepped sideways on her hands. "And I can dance around." Easing herself down to rest, Janie coaxed, "Come on, Courtney, try."

Ms. Rogers stuck her head in the door. "Did you want something?"

"Ahh, yes." Courtney said, having completely forgotten the flashing light.

Janie piped up. "Would you do us a favor? Move the beds closer to one another so we can pass things back and forth."

"Ever hear the magic word 'please,' Janie?" The nurse put down her paperwork.

"Didn't you know," Janie said, trying to look wide-eyed and innocent, "that I'm under strict doctor's orders to only use it once a day. Otherwise, I could get deathly ill."

"Is that so?" Ms. Rogers unlocked the wheels all the way around Janie's bed and then Courtney's. "Sounds like a very serious condition to me." She rolled the beds closer together and up against the wall. "That should do," she said, locking the wheels into place again.

"Thanks," Janie offered. "I'm allowed to say that three times a day."

Ms. Rogers smiled as she straightened the sheets and blankets over the cast. "Are you both comfortable in that position or do you want to sleep on your sides? It's time for bed."

"I'm fine, Ms. Rogers." Courtney managed a yawn.

"Me too."

"If you do want to change during the night, use the flasher again. I'll be in the office." She thrust up the side rails on Janie's bed.

"Hey," Janie griped, "those are for the little kids."

"It's just a precaution, dear."

"Boy, might as well put us in the ward with all the three-year-olds," Janie muttered. She heard Ms. Rogers lifting the rails around Courtney's bed.

"At least they know how to say please," Ms. Rogers chided gently. "Sweet dreams, my friends." She switched off the lights.

"Humph," Janie snorted, "bedrails!" She ran her hand along the cool metal bars, thinking about Ms. Rogers. She was still her favorite nurse.

"Janie, look at me," Courtney whispered.

"Sure," said Janie, peering across the darkness.

Courtney, almost in a vertical position, was

hanging onto the bed rails. "Janie, I can see out the window. It's the most beautiful view ever."

Janie was filled with an unexpected blast of happiness. It was as if a shooting star had exploded inside her chest. She lifted herself up. Almost kneeling, she clung to the bars and touched the sill. Her fingers managed to grab one of the levers and push the window ajar slightly.

"Courtney, they never locked it. We can still get rid of food." Janie let the gentle trickle of night air wash over her face and through her cropped hair. "You know what, Courtney? I think the dragon has finally gone. And spring is coming. I can smell it!"

# 10

It was exactly three weeks later that the policeman stomped off the elevator and made his way,
hat in hand, to the charge nurse's office. Moments later he and Mrs. Bickerstaff appeared
outside the door of 318K. Mrs. Bickerstaff glared
at him, his hat, and the window.

"Janie, there's a policeman out in the hall.
He and Mrs. B. are breathing fire at each other."

Janie reached for the Old Testament. "In the
beginning God created heaven and earth," she
read aloud.

"Janie, we're in trouble. He's pointing this
way! What are we going to do?"

Janie grinned over Genesis. "What can we
do? Here we are, two plaster turtles weighing
in at three hundred pounds apiece—could we

run away? I'd just like to know what we did." She wet her second finger with a lick and turned the pages.

". . . and of every living creature of all flesh, thou shalt bring two of a sort into the ark that they might live with thee."

With clenched fists, Mrs. Bickerstaff headed into the room. "Girls!" she said without looking at either of them, "I am shocked." She paced the narrow path between the beds. Without another word, she marched out of the room and returned with the policeman's hat.

Resting on the regulation cap was a messy heap of poached egg, the hospital dietician's idea of a morning specialty. A little bit of the white lumpy part hung over the peak, resting on the gold shield.

Janie smothered her laughter behind the book. It was only a short time before that her watery eggs hadn't looked like anything she could swallow, so she had heaved them for the birds. The eggs, it seemed, had never made it to the ground.

Ever since they had been throwing food to the pigeons, meals had not been a problem. Their plates were always empty. The nurses didn't complain to the dietician, and she didn't scold them for not eating. And Janie and Courtney lived happily on fresh fruit, ice cream, bagels with cream cheese, and other goodies from their parents' visits.

"All this time, not only have you not been

eating, but you've been discarding food from the window. I am horrified that anyone would do such a thing. It's unbelievable! Do you know how the policeman found you? He said all he had to do was look up. There is debris stuck to the brick and ivy from the ground floor all the way up to this window."

Janie could not keep the laughter down. The thought of all that spinach and egg decorating the building was too much for her.

Mrs. Bickerstaff did a stiff quarter turn and said in a low, angry voice, "I know this is all your doing, Miss. Something will have to be done. I think the two of you should be sep-arated. . . ."

"I hate that food," Janie snapped at the nurse. "It's slimy. I won't eat it. Even the pigeons don't look too great since they've been living on it."

The conversation ended there. Dr. Michaels arrived with a group of interns on morning rounds. Mrs. Bickerstaff gave him a tight smile, glowered at Janie, and returned to the policeman in the hall.

Janie retold the story later, as the doctors looked her over. A young woman teased Janie about giving the pigeons vitamins to restore their health. Janie calmed down once she started laughing.

"But you do have to eat something. When was the last time you had a meal?" Dr. Michaels asked. "We can't have you two dying of starva-tion in a hospital. What would people say?"

Then Janie blurted out that they always had little lemon meringue pies or salami sandwiches after Mrs. Schaeffer's visits. Of course, there were also the bagels and the small containers of yogurt that her own mother smuggled in, but Janie didn't mention that.

"I guess I don't have to worry about you on that diet." The doctor walked across the room.

"No," said Courtney, staring at Janie.

"I think it's time we had some x-rays to see what's going on with you inside there."

"Okay," Courtney said without looking at the doctor.

"How come," Courtney demanded the minute they were alone, "you didn't say anything about the poppy seed cakes from your grandmother? You only told him what my family brings. Now my parents are going to get in trouble. Thanks a lot, Janie."

"I don't think Dr. Michaels will tell. He's our friend. Besides, it's your family that sneaks in all the good stuff. Please, don't you yell at me, too. It's bad enough that Mrs. Battleaxe is always making me feel like a worm that's been stepped on. You know something, she hasn't said one nice word to me since we got here."

"Janie, you shouldn't have mentioned the food. If anyone ever knew what we had in here . . . I don't know what would happen. And Mrs. B. yells at you because you make her cross. Why don't you try saying something pleasant to her first? I bet you haven't said one nice word to her either."

"Yuck," said Janie.

"No, really, why don't you? Maybe it would help."

Janie gulped as if she were going to vomit.

"You won't die."

"I might."

"Maybe no one is ever nice to her and that's why she is so awful."

"Okay, okay." Janie knew Courtney was probaby right. "I'll try, but what I really want to know is, are we still friends even though I blab too much?"

Courtney's face wrinkled up into a funny smile. "You and I will be friends, Janie, no matter what you do!"

"Wow!" Janie smiled. "That's really nice!"


That afternoon, while Courtney was being x-rayed Mrs. Bickerstaff appeared in 318K with two nurses' aides. She clicked off Janie's rented television as the women began gathering Janie's things.

"Hey, what's going on?"

"You're being moved down the hall to a room right next door to my office. That way I can keep an eye on you myself."

Janie opened her mouth to complain but caught herself. Okay Courtney, she thought, here goes. I just wish you were around to coach.

"Mrs. Bickerstaff," said Janie politely, "I'm very sorry about the policeman's hat getting dirty."

At first the nurse did not respond. Finally she said, "It's a little late to be sorry, Dearie."

Janie found herself more annoyed but said nothing. She watched the lady in the pink uniform wheeling her nightstand out the door. It had all her trophies in it. Mrs. Bickerstaff collected the get-well cards on top of the hospital table and laid them on the bed. She was about to open the top compartment of the bedside table when Janie remembered the poppy cakes.

"Ahh . . . ," Janie said quickly, "if I promise never to do it again, could I stay here?"

"There's no way you will be able to do it again, even if you don't promise," the woman replied.

A terrible thought crossed Janie's mind. "Mrs. Bickerstaff, you're going to move Courtney into the same room with me, aren't you?"

The charge nurse turned away to unlock the wheels at the foot of Janie's bed. She didn't say a word.

"Mrs. Bickerstaff?" Janie's voice shook. "I couldn't stand being separated from her. Courtney's my best friend!"

Without looking at Janie she said, "You should have considered that before."

Janie held back from blasting the nurse with her anger. This acting sweet like Courtney wasn't working, but being nasty wouldn't do any good at all. Janie closed her eyes and felt the stinging behind her eyelids.

The bed rolled away from the wall. Janie could hear them struggling to move it through the doorway. She hoped the bed got caught. That would fix them good.

Down the busy hall and into another room, Janie kept her eyes shut. When she heard the wheels being locked in place and the aides leaving, Janie opened her eyes. All around her, black and white owls glared down from their brown wallpaper perches. Talk about feeling spied on, Janie thought.

"Are there any other kids in this room or are you going to keep me in here alone?" Janie dropped her act of pretending to be Courtney. Something, and Janie didn't know what it was, made her realize that no matter how nice she tried to be, Mrs. Bickerstaff would never treat her the way she treated Courtney. And that's okay with me, Janie thought, because I don't like her either.

"I'd prefer to have you stay by yourself, because I think you are a very bad influence on Courtney. But the doctors requested you and she be together so they can study your simultaneous progress. All I can say is that you had better be very careful, Miss, because my office is right next door and I'll be listening to every move you make."

The nurse locked the window. "I've never

in all my years had anything like this to contend with." She stared out. "I can't find anything funny in it whatsoever—"

"But, Mrs. Bickerstaff, could you eat that stuff? It's so gross!"

"This conversation is getting you and me nowhere, I can see that. Let's end it right there. I don't think you have the right to comment on the food. This isn't home and—"

"My father told me I have the right to tell the truth."

"That's enough, Miss Tannenbaum." Mrs. Bickerstaff marched out to answer a phone that was ringing.

"Well, I tried. You saw me try," Janie told the disapproving owls. "She hates my guts." Janie dropped her head onto her fists. "Rats," she muttered. "Rats, rats, rats!"

# 11

---

Janie waited impatiently for Courtney to return
from x-ray. No one had been in to see her all
afternoon.

Probably no one knew where she was. She
might be alone the rest of her life and no one
would find out. Probably starve to death, too.

Janie smiled. What a great idea. She should
go ahead and die. That would fix Mrs. B. Would
she ever get in trouble!

Janie laughed out loud thinking about it.
She'd even leave a note putting the blame on
that creepy nurse. She'd be sorry she ever
messed with Tannenbaum-the-great!

Janie heard the ding of the elevator bell across
the hall, and almost at once could see Courtney
on a stretcher and bossy Mrs. B. directing them

toward 300K. This corner room, Janie suddenly realized, was fantastic for spying, all the way down the hall and into the Babies Ward.

As the stretcher table rolled through the door, Janie was itching to recount her latest run-in with Mrs. Bickerstaff, but she kept her mouth shut. She clicked on the television, and the sound blasted out of the box.

"Turn that thing down, Miss, or I'll have it removed." Janie said nothing, but stuck out her tongue at the departing nurse.

"You wouldn't believe what happened to me," Janie began. "Mrs. Bicker was so mad. . . ."

But Courtney wasn't listening. Instead, she gazed out the window, ignoring Janie.

"Hey, what's the matter? Are you angry with me?"

Courtney shook her head sideways.

"So, what's the problem then?"

There was no response.

"Come on, tell me."

Courtney's voice wavered as she fought back the tears. "The doctors decided to delay my operation, Janie. It had something to do with what they saw on the x-rays.

"What's so bad about that? Maybe you won't need one."

"Oh, yes, I will! I'll probably need ten operations. My scoliosis is much much worse than yours."

"What a showoff! Quit bragging!"

"No, I'm not. I'm just tired of this place. I

want to go home. We've been here so long, it's almost spring."

"Don't you think I feel the same way?"

"But . . . you'll go home and leave me here."

"No way. I'll refuse to leave till you do. And you know what else? Mrs. Bickerstaff is just about ready to throw us out anyway. We'll both be out of here in no time. You wait and see."

"What do you mean?"

"That's what I'm trying to tell you about. Didn't you notice the new room? Bicker blew her stack today, after you went to x-ray. She wanted to separate us—"

"Janie, I'd die if they—"

"That's part of the plan I have for us. If we both died and and blamed her, that would get us out of here. For sure!"

"Janie are you nuts?" Courtney smiled, forgetting her tears.

"But it would work wouldn't it?"


"Suppertime!" Miss Parker sang when she carried in the dinner trays, two hours later. "And," she said merrily, "it's delicious spinach with steamed frankfurters."

"Not again!" both girls moaned together. "Make a wish," they told each other almost in unison. Each closed her eyes and wished hard.

"Spinach is very good for you. It has lots of iron in it. I just love spinach!"

"You do?" the two said at the same time. They wished again.

"How come?" said Janie.

"Why?" Courtney scowled. "Janie, you should have said 'why' not 'how come.' One more wish and we might have gotten rid of the spinach. In fairy tales you make a wish three times, and it always comes true. We might have done it."

Janie had her own ideas about the accursed spinach. "Miss Parker, do you really like spinach?" Janie uncovered the green wilted vegetable and the shriveled hot dogs. The steamy aroma ascended toward the nurse's nostrils.

Janie held her breath so as not to gag. Miss Parker took a big sniff and eyed the dinner tray longingly. "I would certainly eat such a delicious meal. In fact, I wish I had had time to make myself dinner before I came on duty tonight."

Janie covered the plate so the steam could collect under the dome again. "How come you're here tonight?" she asked, making polite conversation. "I thought you only worked during the day."

"They changed my schedule, and my stomach is all mixed-up. I wasn't hungry when I came on the floor, but I'll be starved out of my mind by the time I get off duty."

"There's always the candy machine down the hall," Janie suggested helpfully. "It's really too bad though," she said, pausing for just the right effect, "that all this food has to go to waste. Isn't it, Courtney?"

Courtney had been following Janie's discussion carefully. "It sure is," she said, taking Janie's lead.

"What do you mean?" There was a baffled expression on Miss Parker's face.

"Well, you see"—Janie enunciated her words slowly and distinctly—"Courtney is allergic to spinach. The dietician must have forgotten. And I can't eat hot dogs."

"Why not?"

"Because I'm Jewish." Janie said it as if that had always kept her away from hot dogs!

"Ohh, I see."

"So if you want to, you could probably have a mouthful of spinach to tide you over till later." Janie opened the container of milk and read the label for freshness.

"I really shouldn't do that," the young nurse said, lifting the dome off Janie's plate. She was hit in the face with a steamy blast. "But a little bite wouldn't hurt," Miss Parker said, picking up a finger full. "This is so delicious it really shouldn't go to waste. I'll have to see if I can get you something else. You'll be hungry."

"That's all right." Janie shoved the dinner tray at her. "I don't eat much these days."

"You'll have to promise not to tell anyone," Miss Parker cautioned them on her third mouthful, "or we'll all get in trouble."

"That would be awful, wouldn't it, Courtney?"

"Terrible," Courtney said, nodding her head solemnly.

"I'll tell you what, Janie," Miss Parker said, "if you eat your spinach, and Courtney eats her hot dogs, I'll eat the rest. Okay?"

"Okay," Janie said nonchalantly. She began to cut her vegetable up into bite-size pieces and spread it around the plate. The rest is easy, she thought. She squirted gobs of mustard all over, but resisted decorating the red jello in the round plastic dish.

"Well, I better go," Miss Parker said, checking her uniform for green stains. "Promise you won't tell Mrs. Bickerstaff? She'd have my head."

"I'll never breathe a word." Janie winked.

"I'll bring some extra cookies and chocolate milk for you two when I take snacks around. Okay?"

"Terrific!" Janie and Courtney said together.

# 12

On Monday afternoon, Janie was bored. She did not feel like doing the schoolwork her teacher had sent or reading the books from her father. And Courtney refused to talk; she was struggling over her science homework.

Half-heartedly Janie decided on the television. Nothing good's ever on in the afternoon, she thought, switching the channels with the remote control. But she stopped pushing buttons when she saw a nurse kissing a doctor in an operating room. They were slobbering all over one another and mumbling words about love!

"Oh sure, thought Janie, nothing like that happens around here! Bickerstaff would blast off into orbit if—

"Hey, Courtney you should see this soap

opera! All the doctors and nurses are kissing. You think any junk like that goes on around here?"

"I never saw anything, but I bet it does," Courtney said without looking up.

"You're kidding! You really think so?"

"Janie," Courtney spoke as one of the knowledgeable, "everybody falls in love. That's what you do when you grow up."

"Oh yeah . . . well . . . I'm not falling in love if I don't want to."

"No, silly, you don't fall in love with someone you don't like. You fall in love with someone you . . . love."

Janie thought about that for a while. Wonder who's in love around here. The first person who came to mind was Mrs. Bickerstaff, but Janie dismissed that idea. "Do you think Miss Parker is in love with anyone, Courtney?"

"I don't know, Janie, but would you please let me finish up this chapter. I have to send it back with my mother tomorrow."

"Sure, sorry. I'm going to ask her. She'll tell me."

"You can't do that, Janie." Courtney looked up briefly.

"Why not? What's wrong with that?"

"I don't know," Courtney said. "I just never heard of anyone asking."

"I don't see why not. In fact," Janie said brightly, "I'm going to ask everyone I see if they're in love."

Courtney dropped the book. "That's a fantastic idea. We could ask them why and when and how. And even whom!"

"Wait a minute. It's my idea. A second ago you didn't even want me to ask Parker. Now all of a sudden—"

"Well, of course, you would do all the asking. I'd just write the stuff down. Maybe we could find out what really goes on around here."

"Okay. Make a list of everybody. I want to figure out who loves who."

"It's whom, Janie."

"What?"

"It's 'who loves whom,' not 'who loves who.' "

"I like who loves who better." Janie flipped off the television. "First of all, I want to know if it hurts."

"What?"

"Anybody that I ever saw who was in love looked as if they had a bad stomachache. So I want to know if it hurts."

"That's crazy."

"No, it's not."

"Sure it is. It couldn't possibly hurt."

"How do you know? You ever been in love, Smarty?"

Courtney blushed. "No, but I've read lots of books about love. And not one of them ever mentioned pain."

"Listen, it's my questionnaire. So I can ask whatever I want."

"Okay, okay. Next?"

"How do you know when you're in love?"

"Got it. What's next?"

"Ummm . . . don't you have any ideas?"

"You mean I get to ask some questions?" Courtney ribbed Janie.

"Come on, Courtney."

"How about 'number of times in love' and something about a first love?"

"And which one was the best?"

"You think we should ask that?"

"Sure!" Janie roared. "And—can you love more than one person at a time?"

"That's no good, Janie. Everyone knows you can't."

"Why not? I love my mother and father."

"That's different."

"No it's not. Love's love!"

"You're wrong, Janie. There's all different kinds."

"Oh, yeah? Who said?"

"I don't know, some guy, a long time ago."

"I don't believe you, Courtney. Prove it."

"Ahh . . . all right. I've got one. Do you love your French poodle the same way you love your parents?"

"I hate my French poodle. You lose."

"Janie," Courtney said in exasperation, "you know what I mean."

"All right, all right! I get the drift. Then let's ask 'how many kinds of love are there?' "

"Fine. Now what?"

"Who's your one true love? Does love last forever? Can you fall in love with someone who is already dead?"

"Janie, that's nuts."

"Yeah, I know, but I want to ask."

"But why?"

"Because!"

The haggling over questions went on all the rest of the day and well into the evening. When they finally finished, there were over fifty items on the list, and Janie and Courtney lay in wait for their first victim to come through the door of room 300K.

Janie was ready when Miss Parker brought in their milk and extra snacks. She and Courtney were the only patients on the entire floor having chocolate milk for the third night in a row.

"Hey, Courtney, look who's here! It's Miss Parker, our FAVORITE nurse."

"Hello," Courtney said without looking up from her book. She was not trying to be rude, but she wasn't sure she could stand watching what was going to happen next.

"We missed you at dinner," Janie said, biting into a graham cracker. "Yuck, these things are terrible." She made a face when she swallowed what was in her mouth. "They're soggy. I have some chocolate and peanut butter cookies that my mother brought. They'd go better with chocolate milk. That okay with you, Miss Parker? Courtney, you want any GIRL SCOUT COOKIES?"

"No, thanks." Courtney reached for a writing pad. 'Girl Scout Cookies' was the signal that Janie was about to begin.

"You know, Miss Parker, Courtney and I were talking today . . . about things."

"What things, Janie?"

"Well, growing-up things . . . you know what I mean." Janie tried to look embarrassed.

"Oh." Miss Parker swallowed. "Those things!"

"You're probably one of the only ones we can talk to around here because you're not old and crochety like the rest of the people."

The nurse reached for a cookie and then pulled up a chair. "Shoot!" she said. "What's on your mind?"

Well, here goes, Janie thought. "Are you sure you won't mind me asking you a whole bunch of questions?"

"Janie, I can handle it. You know, I studied to be a nurse."

"What I really want to find out about is . . . love!"

"Love? I thought you were going to ask where babies came from."

"Naa . . . I know all about that. My friend, Harold, told me all about the birds and bees catalogs. He said that you send away for babies, to the same place that has the birdseed."

Miss Parker looked up from wiping the crumbs off her uniform. "Janie? . . . How old are you?"

"Hey, I was only kidding," Janie protested, afraid the nurse might really believe her. "I really want to know if you've ever been in love."

"That's so much easier to answer. Yes, of course."

"What's it like?"

"Well . . . lots of fun, I'd say."

"How'd you meet?"

"I was going around in a revolving door."

"Did you get that Courtney? Revolving door."

"What's going on?" Miss Parker looked over at Courtney's bent head.

"We're writing stuff down to see if we can make any sense out of love."

"What are you going to do with what I tell you?"

"I don't know. Nothing probably."

The worried expression on Miss Parker's face relaxed somewhat.

"What's he like?"

"Who?" Miss Parker asked, watching Courtney scribble.

"Your BOYFRIEND! That's who!"

"Him? Oh, he's very nice."

"Miss Parker, would you like another cookie?"

The nurse looked back at Janie. She accepted another.

"Tell us about him."

"He's about ten years older than me and never been married. . . ." She hesitated. "Are you sure you have to write this out?"

"To tell you the truth, Miss Parker"—Courtney put down her pencil—"Janie and I are doing a scientific study because the whole question of love is so . . . questionable. If you know what I mean. We are only asking a few people that we really trust around here. You, Ms. Rogers, Dr. Michaels maybe. We won't tell anybody what anyone else says. It's to help us, that's all."

Miss Parker nodded. She seemed satisfied.

"And don't you tell anyone either," Janie added. "It will ruin the experiment."

"Okay, I won't. I promise."

"Where were we? Courtney, could you go back and read Miss Parker's last statement?"

". . . older than me, never been married."

"Right. I remember what I was saying. So anyway, he's coming from the Midwest this spring for a visit."

"Do you want to marry him?"

"Yes, but not right away. I want to work and travel for a while."

"Does he want to be married?"

"I think so."

"Suppose he marries someone else?"

Janie noticed an odd expression flash across the young nurse's face. There were funny little twitching wrinkles around her lips, and her eyes sort of twinkled.

That was how Janie described it to Courtney

later on when they were discussing victim number one. "What came after that?"

"Then she said, 'Oh, he wouldn't do that. He loves me.' "

"That's right. Too bad Ms. Rogers walked in then. Parker would have gone on talking all night."

"I think that was the problem, Janie. I heard Ms. Rogers saying that half the hall still didn't have their snacks, and it was already way past bedtime. She seemed annoyed."

"I know. I didn't think she ever got like that. I figured Ms. Rogers was always nice, and You-Know-Who was always horrible."

"I don't think it works that way, Janie. Are you going to ask Mrs. Bickerstaff the love questions?"

"No way. I told you I'm never talking to her again. Besides, what would she know about love?"

"I think you're wrong."

"You ask then. She likes you better anyway. If I tried, she'd probably think I was up to something bad. You do it."

"Okay, I will. Night, Janie."

"Night."

"Janie, one more thing."

"Yeah?"

"What are we going to do with all this information?"

"I'll figure out something. I have a funny feeling this love stuff will be too fantastic to waste."

# *13*

---

For the next three days Janie plagued everyone who came into their room about love. And Courtney wrote it all down.

Mrs. Bickerstaff was a little brusque at first, but she did tell Courtney that she had a husband and two college-age children whom she loved very much.

When Janie cornered Dr. Michaels, he said that he was not in love with anyone right now. He laughed when Janie asked him what being "in love" meant and said he really didn't know for sure himself. He had been in love once with a very beautiful and very wonderful woman but she decided she loved someone else. Janie got the idea from him that love was sometimes hard.

"He had such a weird look on his face, I didn't want to ask him if love hurt. You know, Courtney, this is complicated. No one has said the same thing twice. Look at all the people we asked. Some of the nurses were in love with doctors, others hated them. The dietician said she was married but loved a man who died a long time ago. And that priest guy, he said he loved everyone."

"You still haven't talked to Ms. Rogers yet?"

"Nope. I'm saving the best for last. In the meantime, do you want a poppyseed bagel with cream cheese or an onion with butter? My grandmother said to eat them today."

"No more pumpernickel?"

"All gone."

"Poppy," Courtney said, clicking the flasher on so the nurse would come into their room and make the delivery. "Hide it in something," she said matter-of-factly, picking up a book.

"Right." Janie yanked the one-legged rolling table closer. She lifted back it's top surface and made an ugly face at herself in the inside mirror. Her curly red hair was wild from not being combed in weeks. Janie enjoyed the thought of all those knots. She dropped a hand in and rummaged through her junk: get-well cards even though she wasn't sick, a letter from Harold never answered, fourteen packs of bubble gum, a jewelry box for earrings she wouldn't be caught dead wearing, and frilly blue stationery that stunk like a funeral parlor. Janie hadn't figured out how to get even with the joker who had sent that, but she was working on it.

Janie dumped the stinky notepaper into the table's well. The bagel fit perfectly inside the deep blue box. "Ever notice how long they take to get here when you really want them?"

Courtney said nothing. She was far away in Greno.

Janie munched on the onion bagel and played with the table. She pulled it toward her, then shoved it away. The table rolled easily.

"Hey, willya look at that!" Janie pulled the table toward her again. Maybe she didn't need to call the nurse after all. She thought it over, and then placed the boxed bagel inside.

Now, if she gave it a real hard shove, it should go sailing right across the room. Janie grabbed the table and rolled it back and forth, revving it up for a maiden voyage.

"Courtney, watch this." But Courtney was oblivious to what Janie was doing. This'll shake her up when it bashes into the bed, Janie thought. She thrust the table off with a mighty shove. With a will of its own, the table moved in a crazy zigzag dance and halted no more than a foot from Janie's bed.

"Nuts!" Janie dragged herself down to the bottom end of the bed and reached over the edge, glad the guard rails were down, glad that Courtney hadn't looked up from her reading.

She inched herself out almost to her waist. Bit more practice, that was all she really needed.

As her fingers hit the edge of the rolling table, Janie felt her knees slipping. Too much of her top-heavy weight hung off the bed. Automatically, she locked the other arm around the foot railing, afraid even breathing would topple her onto the floor.

The table trembled under the sweaty pressure of her fingers. "Are you kidding me?" Janie, aghast, asked herself aloud. "Now what are you going to do, dummy?"

It must have been her peculiar tone of voice that made Courtney glance up. "Janie, what are you doing?"

"Killing myself, I think."

Courtney pressed the flasher's emergency button. "Hang on Janie! And don't let go!"

Janie's arm, wrapped around the metal bar, began to ache. She studied the brown floor as if it were the bottom of a ravine. Never in a lifetime of getting in and out of bed had she ever realized how far away the floor could be. The pain was shooting into her shoulder.

From nowhere Janie remembered part of a rhyme. The loose fragments whirled around in her head. "All the king's horses and all the king's men. . . ." Her arm felt as if it were being ripped away from the shoulder socket.

"What's the matter?" Ms. Rogers asked before she saw. "Dear God! Janie!" The nurse grabbed the bars on the cast and shifted Janie back onto the bed.

"If you hadn't come just then I . . ." Janie close to tears shuddered from the pain and the relief.

"It's okay. You're all right. Just relax."

Janie rubbed her sore arm. "Well, that was sure fun," she said weakly.

"Janie"—the nurse flung herself into a chair—"when are you going to learn to be careful?"

"I was just trying to—"

"Janie, I don't care about any of your reasons. You did a very dangerous thing."

"I'm sorry."

"That's not good enough, either. Not if you're going to do something else just as stupid."

"I don't think I will."

"Janie, I'm disappointed. I thought you had a lot more sense than that."

Janie was crushed. What Ms. Rogers said hurt even more than her arm. "I won't do it again. Honest, I mean it. And thank you."

"If you'd fallen, it could have been disastrous. You might have broken your neck or destroyed all the corrective work being done on your spine. You are a wonderfully spirited child, and I love you for it. We all do. But you need to be more cautious and not let your ideas get so out of hand. Do you have any idea of what I'm talking about?"

"Yes," Janie said gruffly. I'm always in trouble at school for the same reason. My teacher says the same thing."

"Promise me you'll never stop being your crazy self even when you're grown-up. But just be a bit more careful, as boring as that may sound to you."

"Okay, I'll try. You're not angry with me anymore?"

"No, I wasn't really angry. You just scared me."

Janie took a big gulp of air.

"Oh, there is one little thing though," Ms. Rogers said, crossing her legs at the ankles and studying the scuff marks on her white shoes.

Janie frowned at Courtney. "What's that?"

Courtney, who had said nothing all this time, looked worried.

"I hear you two have been up to some questionable antics lately."

For a second Janie thought the whole world was going to come crashing in on her again, but Ms. Rogers had an odd expression on her face that made Janie wait another moment.

"It seems," Ms. Rogers went on, "you've been asking everyone questions, and I was wondering how come you haven't bothered me?" Her mocking smile, the one Janie loved best, colored her beautiful face.

"Are you in love?"

"Is that the kind of questions you've been asking? No one is revealing the subject matter of the so-called scientific studies taking place in 300K."

"Are you in love? Yes or no."

"No."

"Have you ever been?"

"Yes, when I was married."

"You aren't any more?"

"Married, or in love?"

"In love and married also."

"No, I'm not in love or married either."

"How come?"

"Is that on the official questionnaire?"

"Not being in love is."

"Well, Janie . . ." The nurse stopped and thought. "I could answer both things in the same way. It just didn't work out."

"Are you sad?"

"No, not anymore."

"Do you think you'll ever marry again?"

"I don't know. Things are different now."

"What do you mean?" Janie had the feeling they were finally close to something that would make sense.

Ms. Rogers smiled. "I guess I let myself in for this, didn't I? Listen, Janie, I can't stay and talk to you, as much as I'd really enjoy doing that. I have work to do. Now, I understand what took Nelly Parker so long the other night. But maybe before you two leave, there will be some time. My official answer for the notorious questionnaire the entire staff is worrying about is that, while love may be wonderful, right now I'm not dying to be in love or married to anyone. And that, friends, is a relief!"

"One more question," Janie begged. "Just one more."

"And this has to be the last."

"Why's it a relief?"

Ms. Rogers, threw back her head and laughed. She laughed her way out the door, and they heard her laughing all the way down the hall.

"That," said Janie, "is what I call weird. I wonder what was so funny?"

"I don't know."

"I don't understand anything at all about love. Ms. Rogers is the prettiest one in this whole place. She should be in love."

"I don't think being pretty has anything to do with it."

"Well, what's it got to do with then?"

"I don't know either, Janie. But it's too bad she isn't in a hospital like you saw on TV."

"Yeah, then some rich, good-looking doctor would be madly in love with her!"

Courtney sighed. She pictured the chiseled profile of some fiercely handsome man gazing into Ms. Rogers' mysterious eyes.

"Courtney!" Janie pounded the bed. "I've got the greatest idea!"

"What? What? Tell me."

Janie hooted. "Suppose . . . just suppose we could find Mr. Medical America for Ms. Rogers? Someone really wonderful and really really handsome. . . ."

Courtney's eyes glowed. "Oh, Janie! I know what you're thinking. But how? How could we ever?"

"Birdseeds!" Janie laughed at her own cleverness. She was already way ahead of Courtney on the Janie-Tannenbaum-Greatest-Scheme-Ever-Campaign!


"Hello there, lady," Dr. Michaels said when he found Janie up on her knees looking out the window. "Are you planning to run away again?"

Janie smiled. He'd never told on them. "No, I was watching the pigeons carrying on. Must be building a nest nearby. Listen to the racket they make, billing and cooing. Isn't love wonderful!" Janie settled down on her bolsters and studied Dr. Michaels' profile. "Ever think much about pigeons?"

"No, I can't say I have, except that they're supposedly dirty and diseased."

"What kinds of disease?"

The doctor sat on the edge of Janie's cluttered bed. "I don't want to talk about pigeons at the moment, not when I have other important things to tell you."

"Like what?"

"We've scheduled your operation for next week. If all goes well, as I expect it should, you'll be able to go home after that."

"Oh! Wow!"

"I'll have a definite date for your parents after

124

the operation. You can spend the summer at home. Then when you come back in the fall, we'll take the cast off. How's that sound?"

"Terrific! Janie glanced across the room at Courtney, hiding behind a history book. "Dr. Michaels . . ." Janie said, not able to cover her uneasy feelings.

He followed Janie's gaze. "Courtney has a ways to go yet."

"That's not fair."

"No, it's not. But sometimes that's how things work."

"She won't have to stay here forever, will she?"

The doctor laughed. "Who said that? Courtney? She'll be fine, Janie." He stood to leave.

Ever since that night he had found her on the back steps, Janie had thought he must be the greatest doctor in the entire world. It has to be him, she decided, and it's now or never. "Dr. Michaels, do you go home at the same time every day?"

"No, why?"

"Listen . . . I need . . ." What do I need? Janie thought. Help, that's for sure. Help! That's it. "Dr. Michaels, I need your help."

"What kind of help, Janie?"

"Ahh . . . well . . . could I whisper in your ear?"

"What's this all about?" Dr. Michaels said, stooping to Janie's level. His chin rested on the frayed cuff of his white uniform smock.

Up close Janie's stomach flopped over. She had to make this thing work.

"Dr. Michaels, I need you to do something for me and Courtney. Can you keep a secret and not ask too many questions? We won't make you do anything bad, just a favor." It was coming out jumbled. Janie gritted her teeth and slowed down.

On one side, Dr. Michaels' lips twisted up higher than the other. "Sounds like a dangerous assignment to me. Can you give me a little more to go on?"

"Sure," Janie took a huge gulp of air. The Greatest-Scheme-Ever was going to happen. And Janie Tannenbaum was doing it. "There's this lady that Courtney and I see outside, all the time. She's very beautiful and mysterious."

"Mysterious? What makes you say that?"

"She's always alone and never talks to anyone, and she wears a long black cape. We call her the Mysterious Pigeon Lady because she feeds the pigeons every single day, even in the dead of winter. One time we saw her out there on a moonlit night. Wait till you see her," Janie said, getting carried away. "What I mean is, Courtney and I have to send a message to her. Would you take it?" Janie finished quickly. Dr. Michaels was looking at her suspiciously. "You wouldn't have to talk; just wait till she reads the note. She might say something."

"Janie, what are you up to?"

"I can't tell you—I mean, nothing." Janie tried

looking wide-eyed and innocent. "We must reach the Mysterious Pigeon Lady before it's too late!"

"Give me the message."

"It's not ready yet. We're still working on it. Could we give it to you in a few days?"

With one eyebrow arched, the doctor nodded.

"Thanks, Dr. Michaels. You're a real pal." She patted him on the shoulder.

The look in his eyes stayed the same. "Somewhere along the line, Janie, I want you to tell me what's going on around here."

"You," said Janie, "will be the first on your block to know. Just as soon as I figure it all out!"

"And what does that mean?"

"Nothing, nothing." Janie's laugh was extra hearty. "I was only kidding!" Now that he was leaving, she couldn't wait to begin work on Plan B.

"What did Dr. Michaels want?" Courtney abandoned her homework, moments later.

"A couple of things. We discussed the Mysterious Pigeon Lady who wanders the face of the earth feeding birds."

"Who's that?"

"Who do you think it is?"

"Janie, I don't know what you're talking about."

"Sure you do. Ms. Rogers."

"I don't think I understand."

"Yes, you do. You just haven't thought about it before. We're going to have Dr. Michaels and

Ms. Rogers meet outside and fall in love, while they're feeding the pigeons."

"Janie are you crazy? How can you possibly pull that off?"

"You watch. But I need your help."

"What do you want from me?"

"You have to write the love letter that the good doctor will take to the beautiful and mysterious pigeon woman, who is seeking her great lost love."

"Is that all?"

"Neat, huh?"

"I don't know if I want to."

"Come on, Courtney. You're going to be a famous lady writer, someday. It'll be good practice."

"Okay, I'll do it."

"Terrific!"

"Janie, is that all Dr. Michaels talked to you about?"

"No, he said I'm having surgery. . . ." Janies' voice faded, watching Courtney's face. It was like seeing cloud shadows passing over a sunny green hill. Her expression grew dark and then light again.

"I knew it," Courtney said very quietly.

# 14

"No! No! No!" Janie ranted over her dinner tray. Her complaints had nothing to do with the lump of cold macaroni covered with thick glumpy sauce or the hard red meatball. "Less mushy or they'll catch on."

"Well, you write it. I give up. Every time I think of an idea, you turn it down. You do it if you're so smart. It's not that easy, Janie."

"I want it absolutely super!"

"I know that."

Courtney and Janie had ceased bothering to apologize to each other around draft seven. They were running out of scented note paper, and it had to be, they agreed, a perfect love letter!

"Could we say something like, the bearer of this message is a friend?"

"Hey, I like that, Courtney. Keep going."

"Please share your seeds for the birds with him . . . dear noble lady."

"Leave out the noble lady stuff, and it'll be fine."

"I want it in there, Janie. It's mine, too."

"Sounds junky. The dear noble lady has to go."

"Who has to go?" Ms. Rogers said as she came through the door. She reached for a thermometer and began shaking it down.

"Where did you come from?" Janie watched Courtney scrambling to hide the blue frilly paper under her sheets.

"I guess I came from the hall, silly. What were you saying when I came in?"

"We were talking about going out," Janie fibbed as fast as she could.

"Now that the weather is warm, it does make you want to go outdoors. I wish there were a way, but this hospital doesn't have any facilities for that."

The compassion in the nurse's voice made Janie feel almost guilty. But then she thought of her greater cause and plunged ahead. "You know what, Ms. Rogers? Remember my crazy friend, Harold, who sent me birdseed because I told him how bad the food was here? If you took it and fed the birds for Courtney and me, that would be as good as doing it ourselves."

"Janie, that sounds like a lovely idea."

"You hear that, Courtney?" Janie yelled at

her friend, hidden once more behind a book, where she had been reading the same sentence over and over again. "We can watch her from the window."

"Janie, you're not going to try and get out of bed again?" the nurse said with some concern.

"No," Janie said, "but if you move our beds closer to the wall, then we can see the street."

"And you're not planning another throwing food out the window number?"

"No way."

"Honestly?"

"Yeah," Janie said, momentarily thinking of what she was up to. "Could I ask you one more special favor? Would you feed them late in the afternoon, before you come on duty?"

"That's easy enough."

"Super." Janie smiled, rather satisfied with the accomplishment of Plan B.

"Now, if there isn't anything else, may I please take your temperature."

"It's your hospital, Lady. By the way, you wouldn't have a long black cape?"

"No, Janie. Why?"

"Just wondering."


For the next two days and nights it rained steadily. Janie and Courtney endured the daily routines that punctuate hospital time with a constant eye on the heavy gray clouds.

On morning rounds, Dr. Michaels told Courtney she would have her operation shortly after Janie. And while the physician and residents discussed Janie's upcoming surgery, she slipped a frilly blue envelope decorated with colored flowers into Dr. Michaels' pocket.

"Under the trees, just before four, next sunny day," Janie said, in her very best cloak and dagger voice.

"Roger." The accomplice understood his assignment. Janie checked off Plan C.

"I love it! I love it! I'm so smart!" Janie was bursting with exuberance when everyone left.

"Oh, Janie, everything's terrific again. I'm so glad. Won't it be wonderful to be home. Will you write me?"

"Yeah, even though I hate writing. You just better write to me, or I'll come over to your house and beat up on everybody."

Courtney laughed. "You know Janie, I don't know anything about you at home. Do you have your own room?"

"I never thought of that. Yeah, I do. And you should see it."

"Tell me."

"It's always a mess. I bet yours is really neat, right?"

"Sort of."

"My mother says my room might as well be a city dump. She never yells at me about it though. She says it's my room, and if I want to live in a cave with all my stuff piled around me, that's up to me. The only trouble is that when we have company, she locks the door so our relatives can't see it. I can never bring my cousins in, and I know they wouldn't care. We have to go down to the family room or outside. That's the one thing I can't change her mind about."

Courtney smiled at the thought of Janie's room. "I'd like to see it. Do you think she'd let me?"

"If you come over for a couple of days, she has to. I bet they straightened it up while I was here. The lady who cleans our house is always talking to herself about getting into my room. It wouldn't be my room if it were all neat and tidy."

"Maybe they didn't, Janie."

"I hope not." Janie sighed. "So what's your room like?"

"It's pale green, the color of celery. And I have really old furniture that used to belong to my great-grandmother. The bed has a canopy over it. And I keep my clothes in a huge trunk that my grandfather used when he traveled around the world. He was a musician. There's also a dressing table with a mirror that I used to play dress-up in front of, when I was little. Just before I came here, I sat at the table pretending I was a famous lady, not playing, just sitting and looking at myself. That seems so long ago."

"Well," said Janie, "we're almost there!"

# 15

On Friday morning the rain finally stopped. Only a few small islands of dirty snow remained scattered about the hospital grounds. Though the trees were bare, the birds sat chirping in the branches, coaxing the buds to burst. It was also the very last possible day for scheming.

"Good morning." Ms. Rogers snapped up the window shades one after another around the room.

"I don't want to be awake," Janie groaned, still half-asleep. "I was dreaming about playing baseball and making homeruns. Why'd you wake me. . . ." She stopped complaining when the medicinal-tasting thermometer slid under her tongue.

"For a little girl, you have big gripes," Ms.

Rogers said, counting the pulse beats in Janie's wrist.

"Hey, what are you doing here?" Janie spoke through clenched teeth that held the thermometer.

The nurse counted a few seconds more, then released Janie's wrist. "I'm filling in for Mrs. Bickerstaff who's at a meeting this morning."

"Can you still feed the pigeons?" Janie asked as the nurse began checking Courtney's temperature.

Ms. Rogers nodded her white-capped head up and down.

"This afternoon?"

"Yes, Janie. And . . . by the way, you'll be happy to know I have a date this evening." Ms. Rogers paused at the foot of Janie's bed.

"What?" Janie thought she was going to split wide open, cast and all!

"I'm spending the evening with a man I've known a long time but never had a chance to become friends with. We've both been too busy, I guess. Your questions forced me to consider what I've been doing with my life. So when I ran into him the other day, I suggested we have dinner together. And today seemed a good time since I'd be free in the evening."

"Swell," Janie managed to say.

"Janie, I expected a different reaction from you."

"I think it's nice," Courtney said as enthusiastically as possible.

"Is there some problem?"

"No, but feeding the pigeons will take longer than you think. Maybe you should cancel the date. See, there are two bags of seeds, and the birds eat very slowly. One seed at a time is all they can handle. I don't think you'll be able to make your date."

"I didn't know that. Why don't I have my friend meet me here, and he can help me? There's the phone again."

"Noo-oo. . . ." Janie's eyes enlarged to twice their size. "Don't do that!"

"Listen, Janie, I have to go answer that. I'll speak to you later." Ms. Rogers rushed away.

"I feel sick, Courtney."

"Me too. This is worse than having an operation."

"Think, Courtney, think. There has to be something we can do." Janie beat the head part of her cast with balled-up fists. It made a dull knocking sound. "What I'd like to do is steal two stretcher beds and run away."

"This is no time for your jokes. We're in for some BIG TROUBLE, and it's all your fault."

Janie burst out laughing. She hadn't heard a word. "We'd look pretty strange waiting for the bus."

"Stop fooling around, Janie Tannenbaum!"

"Maybe, if we put on sunglasses and wigs, no one would recognize us."

Courtney giggled. "I want a curly red wig."

Janie looked at her. "Yeah, and I'll get a blonde one. They'll never know it's us!"

"Janie, I know what we can do! Dr. Michaels will probably be on doctors' rounds this morning. We can just tell him not today."

"Good thinking! I can't believe that now of all times she has a date. That should take care of it, though. Ummm, and here comes breakfast. This is going to be some other kind of day!"

"It won't be long before you can have whatever you want for breakfast. When I get home I'm going to eat big slices of toasted homemade bread with hunks of cheese on it every single day."

"I'll be eating bagels with cream cheese, bagels with lox, bagels with tuna fish, bagels with everything." Janie lifted the dome off her plate. She slammed it down. "Don't even bother looking. I think it's fried eggs and worms."


The panic began to accumulate when Dr. Michaels did not appear by afternoon for doctors' rounds. "I don't like it," Janie said suspiciously.

"Suppose he doesn't come up to this floor today? Then what?"

"Don't say that. He has to."

"But suppose . . ."

Janie groaned.

"Suppose he doesn't, Janie." Courtney kept insisting.

"Oh, Courtney, don't."

"No, wait Janie, I have an idea. Couldn't you ask to see a doctor?"

"Why would I do that?"

"Don't you have any questions about your operation?"

"Hey, that's terrific!" Janie reached for the buzzer.

"What are you going to ask him?" Courtney said after an hour of listening to the intercom paging Dr. Michaels.

"I want to know if I'll feel anything during the operation."

"Eee. I never thought of that. That's horrible."

"I know it. Let's practice so it sounds real." It was the best pastime Janie could think of to stop the panic from rising.

"Excuse me," a voice said from the doorway, "may I come in?"

"Dr. Pix!" Courtney was surprised to see her old doctor-wizard friend. "We thought Dr. Michaels was coming."

"He couldn't. I believe he had an emergency. He called and asked me to stop by. But before I forget, he wanted me to make sure that I gave you a message. He said to tell you he would be able to meet the Pigeon Lady just before four. Does that make any sense to you two?"

Courtney groaned, and Janie said, "If only it would rain for another forty days and nights."

"Well, as long as you understand. Now, let

me answer that question I couldn't help over-hearing. You will feel absolutely nothing, Janie."

"Nothing?" she said, trying to remember her question.

"By the time you reach the operating room, you will be almost asleep. And once inside, the anesthesia will put you out completely. When you wake up, you'll be either in the recovery room or perhaps down here in your own bed."

"Suppose I wake up in the middle?"

"You won't. There will be a person monitor-ing your sleep all the way through."

"How long before I wake up afterwards?"

"You'll probably sleep right through the first day and then sleep on and off the next. You'll be yourself by the third morning."

"Okay," Janie said. "I can't think of any-thing else."

"If you want to know about something, ask one of the nurses to reach me. If not, I'll see you in surgery on Monday morning, Janie."

"Thanks, Doctor."

Courtney and Janie could hardly look at one another when the doctor left. Both knew there was no way to stop what they had started. And they would even be able to watch the fiasco happening.

"I wonder if we could have some anesthesia now, Courtney? I'd like to go to sleep and not wake up till it's all over."

That afternoon was the strangest that Janie and Courtney had spent together. The minutes just seemed to crawl by as they waited, but the hours slipped by too quickly. They wanted the time to pass so the thing would be over, and they wanted the hands on the clock to stop moving so the meeting would never take place.

Courtney talked to her mother half-heartedly about her operation. And Janie agreed to let her grandmother pack up her baseball trophies so there would be less to carry when she left.

Courtney tried to think. Janie played watchdog over the hall. The panic kept right on growing. Each of them wanted and didn't want visiting hours to end. When they were over, it would be time.

At half past three, Janie made a decision. "I can't stand it any longer. I'm going to confess everything, Courtney. Even if Ms. Rogers gets angry, nothing really horrible will happen."

Janie didn't bother to use the buzzer. "Parker," she roared at the nurse coming out the office door. "Find Ms. Rogers. We need her."

"I think she left early, Janie. Let me check." Miss Parker backed out of the room and into the office. "Yes," she said a second later, with the sign-out sheet in hand, "she's gone for the day. Is there anything I can do?"

"I think I'm going to be sick." Janie clamped her hand over her mouth.

"Me too."

"What's the matter with both of you? Did you eat something spoiled? Maybe I better get Mrs. Bickerstaff."

"No!" Janie exploded. "Don't do that. It's okay, really, Miss Parker."

"Janie and I are both having surgery very soon. That's why we're acting weird. Don't bother Mrs. Bickerstaff about us. You know she doesn't like to be annoyed." Courtney rattled on, hoping to convince Miss Parker.

"Are you sure?"

"Yeah," Janie said, not even bothering to cross her fingers.

Eventually Miss Parker left. "I hope she believed us, Janie. All we need is Mrs. Bickerstaff here for the show."

Janie rubbed her chilly fingers over her flushed face. "It must be time."

"I can't look, Janie."

"Neither can I."

"Well, one of us has to. You do it since it was your idea."

"No, I'm too scared."

Courtney raised herself up enough to look out the window. "Janie, she's out there."

"What's she doing?" Janie kept her eyes shut tight.

"She's sitting on the bench feeding the pigeons. And she's all alone."

Janie opened her eyes and braced herself inside the cast. She was almost all the way up when Courtney started squeaking.

"Here comes Dr. Michaels. Oh, Janie, I'm so scared!"

Janie dropped back down on her pillow and

put her hands over her face. "What's happening?"

"Nothing, he's still a long way off, but I know it's him. He's got that same leather jacket on. You know the one."

Janie started lifting herself again. She felt the pressure from the weight of the cast in her upper arms and wrists.

"Oh, no! There's a man walking from the other direction. Maybe he's her date. It might be all over."

Instead of dropping down again, Janie held herself. She was higher than she'd been before, but her eyes were still closed. "What's going on?"

"Nothing."

"What do you mean nothing?"

Just what I said. Nothing! Why don't you open your eyes?"

"Because I can't stand it. C'mon, Courtney," Janie begged, "tell me what's happening. Where's the other guy?"

There was a long silence, then Courtney said, "Oooo . . . wow! I can't believe."

"What? What? Tell me."

"Dr. Michaels kissed her."

"Whaaat?"

"He kissed her, Janie. He walked up and kissed her."

It was then that Janie's arms gave out. "I don't believe it!" she roared, her eyes wide open.

"I saw him."

"You're making it up. You make up fairy tales. He wouldn't just walk up and kiss her. That's nuts."

"Janie, he KISSED her! I was the one watching, remember?"

"He really did? Wow, love at first sight!"

Janie thrust herself up again and peered down at two of her favorite people. They stood side by side, throwing sprays of seed into a friendly spring breeze. Crowds of pigeons scurried over the mushy ground after food. Some took wing on the gentle breeze, gliding upward to their nests hidden in among the vines and eaves of the hospital building.

"They looked so beautiful together!" Janie said with a sigh when the doctor and nurse finally departed. Her scheme had worked. In fact, it was perfect. "We did it, Courtney," she gloated. "I just can't believe he kissed her." Janie smacked her forehead.

"Janie, that's what happened."

"I wonder if she'll go out with him?"

"Hey, wouldn't it be some joke if he was the one she was going out with, and we went through all this. At least we would know it was meant to be."

Courtney settled down on her brown bolster. "You know, it really doesn't make any sense that he kissed her."

"That's what I said. He has to be the one."

"Maybe he's her brother."

"Or worse, maybe he was her old man."

"Her what?"

"Grow up, Courtney, her husband."

"Well, I never heard that expression. Janie, that would be awful."

"Wonder if she'll tell us."

"Tell you what, Janie?" Ms. Rogers stood in the doorway of their room.

"How'd you—" Janie stopped asking. Courtney was too stunned to speak.

Ms. Rogers came in and sat beside Janie's bed. "Okay, you two, what's going on? I want to know why Nathan—I mean Dr. Michaels—is handing me crazy messages and asking me if I'm the mysterious pigeon lady."

Courtney winced and Janie giggled, remembering what they had written. "It all started," Janie began her tale, "when I was watching TV one day."

"I think it was the soap opera," Courtney interrupted nervously.

"And Dr. Michaels looked so handsome with his leather jacket and this doctor was kissing a nurse in the operating room. Not here, on the afternoon soaps." Janie paused to check Ms. Roger's face. She thought she saw an odd twitching around her lips.

"Sounds very complicated," she said.

"And then," Courtney picked up their story, "Janie and I thought . . . you and Dr. Michaels

. . . well . . . that it would be wonderful if you two . . . became really good friends." She couldn't bring herself to say "fell in love."

"Ahh-ha." Ms. Rogers pulled a crumpled piece of blue paper from her pocket. "Dearest Lady," she read, "Friend of the Noble Pigeon, will you share your magical seeds with the bearer of this message? He—"

"Stop!" wailed Courtney, "I can't listen to that thing."

"And I'm beginning to understand a lot of things like the questionnaire and the birdseed . . . and the long black cape. But this is all so silly. You have no idea—"

"I knew it," Janie hooted, flapping her elbows against the cast. "He's the one you have the date with."

"No, Janie. Not Dr. Michaels. I'm very flattered that you were so concerned, but Nathan and I have known each other for years."

"That's why he kissed you. Are you guys in love already?"

"Janie, Janie, wait! Dr. Michaels and I are friends. We are not in love though."

"Why not?" Janie demanded in disbelief.

"I don't know, except that it never happened."

'Didn't you want it to?" Janie insisted.

"No . . . I guess I didn't." Janie opened her mouth with the next question, but the nurse ignored her. "Janie, listen to me. There is something you haven't learned yet. It's wonderful that you and Courtney wanted us to be in love. I'm sure you did everything you possibly could to make it happen. But love is what two people create between themselves. You can't set it up for them. It has to be their own doing."

"That sounds too simple," Courtney said, dismayed.

"But it's not easy, Courtney, dear." Ms. Rogers stood. She lingered a moment, bent and kissed Janie, then Courtney. "Don't worry about it. See you tomorrow."

After a long silence, Janie spoke, "I still don't understand."

"Maybe it's another one of those dumb things you can't figure out till you're grownup." Courtney was up on her knees. "Look, there she goes."

But Janie didn't bother.

Eventually Courtney eased herself down into a horizontal position. "What's the matter, Janie?"

"Nothing."

"Are you upset because the Greatest-Scheme-Ever-Campaign didn't work?"

"Yeah, I guess so."

"Janie?" Courtney hesitated, "have you ever been in love?"

"How could I if I don't even know what it is? What a question!"

"Ever kiss anyone?"

Janie snorted. "Yeah, me and old Harold had this long talk one time, and we decided to see what the big deal was, anyhow."

"What did you do?"

"I kissed him for a while and then he kissed me. It was pretty disgusting."

"Honest?" Courtney said, rather amazed. "When was this, Janie?"

"Second grade, when we were out in the woods smoking cigars."

# 16

---

The weekend slipped away into hospital routines. Temperatures, bedpans, breakfast, lunch,
naptime, visiting hours, dinner, bedtime. The
days were like so many others, it was impossible
to take special notice of their passing. Time
blurred into one long present moment.

"Hey, do you have anything I could eat?"

"Janie you're not supposed to have anything
the night before."

"But I'm so hungry. I'll probably die of star-
vation not heart failure on the operating table
tomorrow."

"Janie, don't say that!"

"Well, then, gimme!"

"Nice talk, Miss Tannenbaum." Courtney

laughed. "Janie, remember the first day in the bathroom?"

"Yeah, that was pretty funny." Janie relished the memory.

"I didn't like you much. You were so wild and loud, showing off all the time."

"I still am."

"But you're different too."

"How?"

"When I saw your face, looking over the stall, it was just a face I didn't know. Anybody's face. And then one day I saw that you had hazel eyes, and another day that you had a nose with freckles. And each time I found out something new, I saw you a little bit more. It was like putting together a puzzle. I really like your face, Janie. That's why I don't think love has anything to do with being pretty. It's being able to see, or something. Does that sound weird?"

"No . . . I sort of know what you mean. Somewhere I stopped thinking you were stuck-up and prissy. You know what . . . I never thought of this until now . . . I stopped thinking how beautiful you were."

Janie laughed suddenly. "And you know what else, Courtney? One day I noticed you had this scar on your earlobe, and I decided you weren't so perfect after all. Anybody who's decent has at least one good scar."

"You really are my best friend, Janie."

"Well, you better give me something to eat then. Or I'll die on you."

149

"Janie don't. Promise me."

"Hey, I was only kidding! How dumb do you think I am?"

"I know but promise me. Say Teddy Bear."

"Teddy Bear."

"Say it all."

"Say it all."

"Janie, I mean it!"

"Okay, okay. I, Janie Tannenbaum, promise 'Teddy Bear,' not to die tomorrow. NOW can I have something to eat?"

"Listen, Janie, there's one other thing I want to tell you in case . . . I don't know . . . maybe I won't get the chance later."

"This better be good."

"When you leave the hospital, you take the bridge, right?"

"Yeah."

"When you're riding over, there's a castle you can see, way at the top of a hill. It's my castle, Janie. When I grow up, I want to buy it and have all my friends come and live with me. That probably sounds dumb, but I love castles."

"Can I visit, too?"

"Of course. In fact, it will be the only castle to ever have a baseball field."

"Hey, that's pretty neat. Thanks. I could teach you how to play. Why don't you try throwing a few oranges or something to me just for practice now?"

"Okay. I'll find some food for you if you'll answer one more question for me."

"Shoot."

"Question first, then food."

"All right! All right!"

"Janie, are you scared about tomorrow?"

"Naa. . . ."

"Not at all?"

"Nope!"

"Oh, Janie, you're wonderful!"

When the third orange hit the floor, Janie grunted. "This is more like feeding time at the zoo." She grabbed the pear on the fifth try. "I'm so out of practice Harold'll kill me."

"I don't have to, if I don't want to," Janie protested as her cloudy sleep was parted early Monday morning.

"You must take another sedative," she heard a voice saying from far away. "You'll be going up to the operating room very soon."

What seemed like hours later, Janie's legs scraped over the rough bedsheets. Unfelt hands lifted her by the side bars on the cast and placed her face-up on a stretcher table. She heard the metal locks on the end of the straps thud against the cast and then click one into another, belting her down.

As the table rolled through one corridor after another, Janie tried counting the ceiling lights that stabbed at her and flashed overhead. She kept forgetting which number she was on.

I want to see the operating room, she thought,

fighting off the drowsy feeling behind her eyes. She began reciting her own name to stay awake, hardly realizing that it was dark and cool in the hall where the stretcher came to a halt.

Outside the wooden swinging doors, Janie waited, falling into a deeper and deeper relaxation. Then finally, when she was about to drift off, she felt the table lurch and bump over a doorjamb.

She stared blankly around at blue-tiled walls. The ceiling was miles away. Faces hung suspended in midair, peering down at her.

A voice behind a green surgical mask and cap, spoke. "I'm going to put this cone over your face, and I want you to take big breaths, very slowly."

Janie fought back. She didn't like the smell of the black rubber cone. My name is Janie, she told herself, resisting sleep. My name is Janie and you can't get me. Janie. Janie. Janie.

"Now breathe deeply."

My name is Janie. Jan . . . nie . . . Ja— Then everything began to swirl around and around, like music. And the circle went black like a tunnel. Around and around and down, through a long, soft darkness, chasing a thin ray of light, without a way or the desire to come back.

# 17

And after that there was no time. Janie floated in and out of sleep, punctuated by a dull throbbing pain between her shoulders. The rooms changed. Her parents were sometimes there, then gone. Familiar voices drifted nearby, like friendly breezes.

Janie dreamed. Baseballs and bats. Harold's face. Frogs with emerald eyes in wizards' caps. Courtney with enormous swan wings.

Forty-eight hours later, Janie was still a little woozy when she opened her eyes. But like her dreams, the pain and nausea had evaporated. The first thing she focused on was an interesting greenish-yellow mark on her upper left arm. It was a neat bruise. She wondered what she had done to deserve it.

"Good to see your eyes open, again. It's been quiet around here."

"Hi." Janie smiled at her favorite doctor. "What did I do to the guy who gave me this?" Without much strength, Janie held up her sore arm.

"That's from the intravenous."

"What's that?"

"While you were under sedation, we fed you glucose and water. It went into one of the veins in your arm."

"Sounds like what they eat in Greno."

"Hmmm?" said the doctor.

"Oh, that's Courtney's—where is she?" Janie moved her head around slightly. That hurt too.

"Up on the surgical floor."

"When will she be back?"

"Can't say for sure." The doctor's voice was guarded. He changed the subject. "How are you feeling?"

"Yucky."

Dr. Michaels nodded. "I know. But in a few days you'll be up to your old tricks. And you'll be able to go home very soon, now. I'm afraid we'll have you back in school in the fall."

"That's okay with me. But you know what? School seems like something I dreamed about once."

"That happens Janie, but you'll feel the same way about this place one day."

"Dr. Michaels    . is Courtney all right?"

The doctor's gray eyes stared down at Janie,

his lips pressed together tightly. "Yes and no. She's had one operation. She needs a second. . . .

Poor Courtney, Janie thought later on. She was right about her scoliosis. And I wasn't even listening. I called her a showoff, Janie remembered miserably.


The following Monday, Janie looked out the window, unhappy in spite of the sunshine. It had been a long day of waiting, and there was nothing she wanted to do and no one she wanted to talk with.

Outside the first green fuzzy buds clung to the trees. It looked chilly. She wondered if fresh air and grass still smelled the way they used to. At least she'd be home, even if she were in the dumb cast and couldn't go out to play baseball.

A feeling of guilt rushed over her, and her eyes shifted to Courtney's empty bed. Pressing the palms of her hands against her eyes, she fought to stop the tears. Everything'll be okay. She'll be back from surgery soon, Janie kept repeating to herself.

She couldn't figure out why the tears kept coming, but it hurt. All over she was hurting, and the pain was not in her body but in her head. Tell yourself something happy, she thought, not looking across the room. Tell yourself about tomorrow.

In the morning her parents would drive over

the bridge and into the city to take her things home. She'd be riding home in an ambulance. Two whole days early. Janie wanted to feel happy about leaving, but she didn't. The doctors had said there was no reason to keep her any longer. Rubbing her streaked face and runny nose on her arm, she bit her lip and pressed the buzzer, hoping Ms. Rogers wasn't at the far end of the hall.

"Yes, Janie?" The nurse stuck her head in the door five minutes later.

"When's Courtney going to be back from her operation? Today?"

"Janie . . . nobody told you?"

"Told me what?" Janie's voice was shrill.

"They had to delay the second operation for a few days."

"But I'm leaving tomorrow. I won't get to say goodbye. And she's my best friend!"

"Nobody told me you were going home. Did you find out today?" Ms. Rogers' face was etched with her own feelings. "You should be happy," she said, but it sounded hollow.

Janie nodded. Her lip was trembling again. "Bickerstaff told me the doctors said there was no reason for me to stay on." The tears slid down her cheeks, and Janie didn't even try to fight them. "Won't they even bring her back here?"

"Oh . . . Janie, Janie," Ms. Rogers said, crossing the room. She unlocked the tightly fisted hands and held them in her own. "I know, I know. It's so hard."

"I don't want to go home. Not yet. I promised I'd stay till. . . ." Janie sobbed.

"Look at me," the nurse said, lifting Janie's quivering chin. "This is a hospital. And hospitals are only for people needing special medical attention. You know that. For the time being, you're well and don't require care. Courtney does . . . they're keeping her upstairs under observation . . . she's not going home when you are, Janie."

"But it's not fair. I can't even say goodbye. I don't want to go."

"Janie, listen. It's time for you to leave. The hospital needs the bed for another patient. You and Courtney will see one another if you want to. Real friendships go on, Janie. Leave her a note, and I'll see that she gets it. . . . You know what else Janie? If you don't actually use the word goodbye, then you'll never really have parted. And when you see one another again, it'll be just like always."

# 18

It took Janie a long time to actually pick up the pencil and note paper. Writing what she felt made her even more uncomfortable. Just before lights out, she began scribbling down her thoughts on the last of the frilly blue stationery.

*Dear Courtney,*

*I don't know what to say. You're the writer not me. I feel terrible going home without you. It's like a dirty trick. But I can't help it. They won't let me stay.*

*I'll miss you. You're better than any best friend I ever had. More like a sister.*

*There's something else I have to tell you. I think I told you a lie the other day, but I didn't know then. I said I wasn't scared, but*

*I have been. Not so much for me, but for
you.*

*And being scared for you hurts, but I al-
most don't care because it's got to do with
being good friends. I finally figured out,
for myself, what love is about. So if it
doesn't sound too weird, I love you, Courtney.*

*J.T.*

Janie hoped what she was trying to say made
some sense. She didn't understand it completely.
Scribbling her address and phone number on the
back, she shoved the note into a lacy envelope
and gave it to Ms. Rogers.

Janie slept fitfully through the night. When
she finally dropped into a deep slumber it was
almost dawn. A nurse stood by her bed for a
few moments watching the gray sky turn blue,
then she put a package wrapped in crumpled
magenta paper on the bed.

When Janie awoke, she felt fine. There was
the usual morning routine, complete with a rot-
ten breakfast. Janie poured orange juice in the
hot oatmeal and stood the bacon up in her glass
of milk. She tortured the eggs. "Take that. I'm
going home, today!"

Her parents arrived to carry out the two
months' worth of junk she had accumulated.
"My gawd," her father said on his third trip
out to the car, "we'll have to buy the house next
door."

"The exercise won't kill you, Andy-boy," Helene Tannenbaum said, laughing at him.

The ambulance stretcher arrived while the Tannenbaums were out in the hall thanking the nurses. Janie was lifted onto the rolling tablelike bed.

"What's that pink thing on my bed?" she asked as the table began moving away.

The attendant picked up the package and handed it to Janie. "Okay, you guys, let's get this show on the road."

When the ambulance took the approach to the bridge, Janie remembered the pink package that had been on her bed. She tore the wrapping away. Inside was a small silver-colored castle.

Janie had just a moment to see the stone castle out the window of the ambulance before it flashed out of sight. When she looked down at the castle again, she found a piece of white paper tucked inside. The fine delicate handwriting said, "Don't forget Greno. I love you too! CAS."

Janie took a big deep breath and watched the cars whizzing by the ambulance. She had almost forgotten to look for the castle, but how could she ever forget Greno. She'd write first thing tomorrow and send bubble gum for the entire floor. "Hey," she yelled to the driver, "put the siren on will ya? I want my friend Harold to know I'm coming home."